Truth

Aphra Wilson

Published by White Fern Publishing

ISBN 9798709036437

To all the Claire's and Christine's I've ever know.

CHAPTER ONE

1

Anna

Anna stubbed out the cigarette as steps approached, slid the glass ashtray under the sofa, forced the smoke from her chest and flapped her arms around. As the first lock turned, she jumped to her feet and plumped the cushion to hide her day-long body-shaped indent. She ran to the sink as the second lock clicked and turned the hot tap on just as Claire pushed the door open with two heavy shopping bags.

"Hey, I was just doing the dishes. How was your day?"

"It was good. I think the boss likes me more now I got that report in order for him."

Claire raised an eyebrow, "Did you finish work early?"

"Here, let me take that." Anna buried her face in the bag and mumbled, "It wasn't on today, they are going to phone me, when they need me, it was too quiet or something like that." She picked a tin of tomatoes out and became engrossed in the label, avoiding eye contact with Claire.

"That's a shame. I thought it was a busy place. You were getting on well, weren't you?"

"Aye, of course. They will probably call tomorrow. Don't worry about it." Anna crouched at the bottom cupboard, faking interest in its contents, thinking of a diversion to stop her digging any deeper.

The phone began to ring, to Anna's relief.

"That will be your work; you get it!" Claire said.

Anna clasped her hands together in mock prayer and shook her head, she hated answering the phone. She mouthed, "Please, you do it?"

Claire picked up the receiver and greeted the caller with her best office voice. "Good evening, how can I help you?" she listened, then shook her head at Anna, who pretended to look disappointed. Claire waved her away from the kitchen with a smile.

"Auntie Jean! How are you? How are the boys?" she untangled the long curly wire as she took a seat on the stool at the breakfast bar.

Anna sat on the still warm sofa, pulled her knees up to her chest, and began flicking between the five channels; she'd have time for at least one episode of something while Claire was talking to Jean. She secretly wished no one had their number, but Claire trusted her aunt to keep their whereabouts secret. Anna could hear the usual short sentences from Claire's side. It always took a while for her to get a word in between Jean's. Then the phone clicked. The call was over already, Anna listened for Claire calling her back or another ring, presuming they'd been cut off. Something felt off. She muted the TV. Heavy silence filled the flat.

"Everything ok?" she called. "Claire, what is it?" She waited; the hairs on her arms began to stand on end.

Claire moved slowly, rubbing her forehead.

"What is it?" Anna asked, her voice calm,

seeing Claire stress.

"I need to tell you something. My auntie. She wanted me to tell you. She saw someone, she's seen him twice. She wasn't sure the first time. So she went back, and it was definitely him."

"Davie? Is he looking for me?"

"No, not him! Why do you even care about the idiot that left you in all that trouble?"

"Tell me who then! You're making me guess! Is it Bazz?"

"No, he's still in jail, you know that! Look, I don't know how to say it."

"Just spit it out, is it Archie? Or that pikey? Is it someone I need to worry about?"

"No, it's not bad. Well..."

"Whoever it is, it's miles away, and they don't know where we are, so does it even matter? Just spit it out!"

Claire sat down, clenching her hands together till her knuckles were white.

"It's your Dad. He's back."

Anna's jaw dropped, and her eyes widened. "My dad? Andy McVay? Back home?"

"Yeah, he was with Christine, she went back, it's definitely him."

Anna pulled her hands out of the jumper sleeves and placed her bare feet on the floor, she pulled herself to the front of the sofa.

"We need to go, I need to see him!"

"Oh no, no way, we can't go back there!" Claire wrung her hands together, they were now sweating.

"I have to! I thought he was dead, he's come back for me."

"We can't. It's far too dangerous. You cant be seen within 100 miles of the place, there's probably a bounty on your head!"

"No one will see us. We can just go to Christine's."

"Us? I can't go, the police still want to ask me about what happened in my house that night. I can't get arrested!"

"Bazz is in jail. He's taken the blame, the police are happy with that. They aren't looking for us now. Come on. I need you! You can see your auntie and the kids."

Claire's eyes fill with wobbly tears. A big one escapes and rolls down the side of her nose.

"I want all that behind us. I don't want to drag it all up again. It's too dodgy, Archie and the pikeys will bloody kill you if they catch you!"

"Look, I'm going, I've not seen my dad for years. I need to know why. Why he left, why he never got in touch. I need to go!"

"What about work? You might lose your job? We don't have much money left, you canny afford to get sacked this time." Anna narrowed her eyes, knowing Claire was clutching at straws, they both knew Anna had never prioritized work over, well, anything.

"This is a lot more important than a crappy job." Anna stood and walked into her bedroom.

"Do you really think this is a good idea? There are a lot of people after you." Claire followed behind.

Anna stuffed jeans and socks into her rucksack,

"That's not important now. What's important is my dad wants to see me. I'm going now. Go and get ready."

Claire stood in the doorway, biting the side of her lip. "I don't know if he does. She didn't actually say that."

Anna swept the entire surface of her dressing table into the open rucksack, including a hairbrush, kirby grips, mascara, and an empty quavers packet. She stopped and stared at Claire. "What do you mean? Of course he wants to see me. Why else would he go back there now?"

Claire nodded gently, "yep, you're right. He must want to find you." She sighed, and her resistance dissolved. "We can only stay one night, though."

"Yes! Thank you! Pack a bag, and I'll phone a taxi to the train station. We need to get there quick." Anna pulled the bag onto her shoulders, wiggled her feet into her knotted trainers, and skipped to the phone.

Claire walked behind her, shaking her head in the darkness of her room before turning on the light. She began folding a neat change of clothes for the trip.

Christine

Christine had been stirring the same cup for too long. She circled the spoon slowly, watching the side profile of the girl sitting by the window. The low winter sun caught the ends of her long eyelashes, highlighting her cute little nose and perfect cupids bow. The soft downy hair glowing around her forehead made her look otherworldly.

So familiar, yet completely new.

The little face turned to her. Realising she'd been staring, the spoon clattered off the china cup, breaking the spell.

She picked up one mug, then stretched her fingers around the other two handles; she brought them over to the table between her guests. She handed the extra milky half cup to the little girl and pushed the other towards Andy.

"So, you've been here 24 hours now. Are you going to give me an indication of how long your planning to stay? Or what you came here for?"

He sipped the tea and coughed, a deep guttural cough that seemed to shake him from his feet upward.

"Like I said, not long, a day or so. For old times sake, that's all. Showing the young one a bit of her old dad's history."

"Aye, you said that. But I'm just not buying it, pal. I've known you longer than most. You do nothing for old time's sake. If you did, you'd have kept in touch with Anna before now."

"I'm here now Chris, and I'm trying to do the right thing."

Christine sighed, his timing was terrible. "Any time in the last five years would have been great, but no. Here you are six months after she's gone."

The young girl with shiny brown hair that hung from her shoulders like a scarf stared out the window, listening to it all, reacting to nothing.

"Every time the phone rings, I think it might be her, but it never is. No one's heard a thing since she left. She must be having the time of her life out there."

"Did you know her boyfriend? The guy she went with?" he asked.

"Davie, aye, I knew of him anyway. He's an idiot, but you can't tell that lassie anything. She knows best."

Andy smiled and stifled a cough, "Like her mum then." The cough erupted through his fingers.

Christine laughed a little, and her eyes crinkled at the corners. "Very much so."

Andy stood up to pull a hankie from the pocket of his chinos, he continued to cough till he had no more to give. He looked exhausted as he used his arm to lean against the window frame.

"That's some cough you've got there pal.

You had that checked out?"

The girl broke her stillness and looked up at him. He separated the blinds with his finger and thumb and peered through.

"It's just a chest infection, nothing serious." He widened the gap and tilted his head to the side.

"Who lives next door now? The garden's really coming along since we lived there. Look at the size of the apple tree."

Christine was perched on the arm of the sofa, holding her empty mug in her hands. That's old Gina. She's aff her heid. We've had a few run-ins, but she keeps herself to herself these days."

"Really, what kind of run-ins?"

Christine knew he was distracting her from digging any deeper, but she did love a good story. "Well, when she moved in, I still had Gizmo. My old cat. Remember him, big ginger tom?"

"Eh, aye, big ginger cat, aye." He clearly had no idea. The girl was watching Christine intently, waiting for the rest.

"Well, he just did what cats like to do. He shat in her flower beds and scratched about in the mud, and you know what she did? She sprayed him with the cold hose, old witch that she is."

"The cat was digging in the garden?"

The girl looked up at Andy.

"Aye, that's all he did. She soaked the poor wee guy. He was traumatized. So, I went roond, had her by the throat, and I told her..." Christine squeezed the mug in one hand, imagining it was Gina's neck, and pointed to it with the other "If you ever do anything to my wee Gizmo again I'll fucking kill ye."

The girl giggled at the sight of Christine threatening a mug.

"Is she a keen gardener? Does she, you know, plant things?" Andy asked in an overly nonchalant tone.

"What? I don't know. Why do you care? It's my Gizmo, God rest his soul, that you should be worried about. No her scabby petunias."

Andy laughed at Christine's rant,

"So you're not the best of friends then? You don't go out together or anything?"

"Pft, not likely. She's bingo daft. You wouldnae catch me down there throwing ma money away. And no, we are nae best pals. We might say hello now and again if we accidentally bump into each outside, but

I'll never forgive her for what she did to ma wee cat."

"Bingo? Is there bingo round here? When's that on?"

"Right. That's enough. I know what you're doing. You're asking me all these daft questions to stop me from asking you any more. You're no interested in the bingo, or that wummins gardening, so stop talking rubbish."

"Ah, you got me Chris, you cannae kid a kidder."

Christine stood up, pulled her jeans tight, zipped her fleece up to her chin, and swiped all the cups off the table.

"And don't you forget it, McVay. You don't want to tell me any more, that's fine. You can stay the weekend, but that's it. I've got things to do, and people to see." She put the cups in the sink, and turned back in time to see the tail end of a silent conversation between the two.

Anna

Blurred orange and white lights sped behind the glass, Claire leaned on her rucksack, and Anna drummed the table between them with her fingers.

"Do you think he'll recognize me?"

"You've not changed that much; of course he will."

"Do you think we are doing the right thing?"

"No, not at all. This is crazy, the last thing we should be doing is speeding towards that town, in the dark, with no idea what's waiting for us." Claire shook her head and a nervous laugh escaped.

"A bit of me wants to get off at the next stop and go back home. What if he doesn't want to see me?"

Claire sat up, squeezing her fingers so tight the skin squeaked, "I didn't even want to do this, but we're halfway there, if you want to call it off, do it now, so we can get home tonight."

The drink trolley trundled its way towards them, stalling the decision. Anna caught the eye of the woman pushing it.

"Four of those mini bottles of white wine, please."

"None for me. I'm not drinking." Claire

added. The woman looked back at Anna.

"Four of those mini bottles of white wine, please," she repeated with a smile.

As the trolley rattled down the carriage, Anna unscrewed the top, sniffed it, turned up her nose, then gulped it as quickly as the tiny neck allowed.

"Use the cup she gave you," Claire said, pinching the brow of her nose and exhaling a stream of air. "Look, I'm serious; if you have any doubts, let's get off in Perth and jump back on the first train in the opposite direction."

"I just want to see him, I think." Anna wiped a dribble of wine from her chin.

"We don't know who we might bump into. What if Archie catches up with you? Or Ronin, or, what if..."

"Calm down, remember what you're supposed to do? Breath deep, right into your belly, slowly. That's it slow down."

Claire put her hands on her heart, "What if the police see me, they are going to want to grill me about that night. I can't..."

"Breathe slower, wiggle your toes, now tell me five things that you can see." Anna tried to sound as soothing as possible.

"Oh shut up, and give me that cup," she

held the thin white plastic in her shaking hand and held it out for Anna to fill with wine.

"It will be ok. It's just one night. I just have to see him, that's all." Anna said, opening the next bottle.

"I know, I know it's important. We all need our family. Even though I'm terrified, I am looking forward to seeing Jean and the bairns."

"Wait, I'm just interested, that's all. I've got questions, but I don't need him. I've not had a family for a long time. I don't need one now."

Hillary

"Move over!"

"If I move any further, I'll be on the floor."

Hilary Evans tutted and tried to turn around, "Ow, what on earth is that jabbing into my leg?"

The caravan swayed as she wriggled and moaned, reaching down to the source of the pain.

"More straw. It's like living with a bloody scarecrow." She pulled the blanket tight around her shoulders and faced the wall, dragging the last corner of blanket from Ronin's thin grey body.

He gripped the edge and yanked as hard as he could, unfurling the cozy woman beside him and spilling out a rage she hadn't seen before. From between clenched teeth he spat the words, "You'd be on the street if I didn't take you in here, you spoiled cow. Now shut your mouth and go to sleep!"

She lay on her back, listening to his breathing, watching a drip of condensation gather momentum on its way down the aluminium framed window. She thought back to the times she'd thought were hard last winter. An ill horse, a missed beautician's appointment, forgetting to take the turkey out of the freezer on Christmas eve. She could never have imagined a year later she'd be squeezed into a damp caravan, that looked like a prop from a Mr. Bean episode with an illiterate Neanderthal with permanently dirty fingernails.

She lay weighing up options, as she did most nights. There was nothing new. She still hadn't told Daddy what had happened. They hadn't spoken since she married James 6 years earlier. He'd sold her favourite horse and turned her stables into a snooker hall as a punishment, and she'd never gone back. She couldn't very well turn up now, cap in hand, and admit that he'd been right all along.

She had no friends anymore; James had seen to that. All her uni pals had been alienated a long time ago. Her acquaintances from the golf club hadn't looked her in the eye since Pearl and Harriet saw her with this brute.

No, this was her lot until she could figure out a plan. She turned carefully towards the back of his square head. She reached a warm hand into the waistband of his boxer shorts, she was going to make the most of what she had. She placed a breathy kiss on the back of his neck, inhaling the dirty smell. Her hand moved over his cold hip bones and down towards the heat. He heaved air into his chest and began to stir. He jabbed a hard, fast elbow into her soft breasts. "Get yourself to sleep, I told you!" He swung his legs onto the floor, pulled on a jumper from the floor, and stamped the two steps across the tiny caravan. He swung the flimsy door open and stormed out into the darkness. As it slammed it shut, she bit her knuckle with frustration.

No money, no house, and now, no bloody satisfaction. That's all he was good for, and not even particularly good. It was just hard and fast, but it took her mind away from her awful predicament for a few minutes.

Shortly after came a soft rattling knock, which she ignored. He'd have to do better than that. Then fingernails tapped the window, followed by a whisper, "Can we come in? Hillary! Are you awake?"

She wrapped the duvet around her naked body and opened the door a fraction.

"Girls, what are you doing out at this time?"

"We just saw Ronin at the horses. Can we come in? Just for a smoke, then we'll go back to our own van."

With her finger to her lips, she held the door open for Tina and Maria; they were not dressed for December night. She struck a match and lit the candle. By the flickering light, she could see them both shiver with blue lips.

All three sat on the bed. Hillary spread the duvet over the young girl's knees and put her hand out for a cigarette. She hadn't smoked since uni, but these days her little secret vice was her only bit of excitement.

"So, where have you girls been tonight?" she took a long drag, listening to the hot crackle of the burning tobacco. The girls visibly relaxed as they warmed up.

"The Nags Head, then the club. It wasn't great though. No decent boys were out tonight." Maria sounded deflated.

"No decent boys are ever out!" Tina laughed.

"And there are none at home either girls, that's just one of life's little lessons."

"What's Ronin marching about in his pants and wellies for?" Maria giggled, "He's always marching about in a bad mood these days."

"Aye, since everyone in the family found out that Anna stole all his money."

"He's very embarrassed, you know. It was a dreadful thing for her to do to him."

"My uncle said she's just like her Dad. Apparently, he conned Grandad out of a lot of money."

"Yeah, my dad was going to kill him years ago, but he disappeared."

"My Auntie said blood will be spilled if she ever sees Andy McVay again."

"Hmm, a very untrustworthy lot." Hillary popped the cigarette end out of the window. "Not like you lot, eh? Fine upstanding citizens only in this proud family."

Tina put on her poshest voice, "Indeed, my good friend Hillary, you are correct."

"Right girls, it's getting late; grumpy Ronin will be back soon, so on your way!"

After the girls shut the door behind them, she blew out the candle and curled up under the duvet. She fell asleep as she usually did, thinking of a way out of this cold caravan.

Anna

"Oh my god! Come in, come in, I've missed you so much!" Jean held Claire's head between her big hands and kissed her forehead a hundred times. "The boys have waited up for you, Boys! She's here, come down and see your big cousin!"

They all shuffled into the hallway, sliding plastic tools and metal cars out of the way with their feet. The twins thundered down the stairs and overwhelmed Claire's tiny body.

"Are you babysitting us?" One asked, then the other followed with,

"Can we play Lego?"

"Do you want to watch round the twist?"

"Let her in for a seat. On you go, into the living room!" Claire and the boys disappeared behind the door in a swarm of bodies and laughter.

Anna followed, but was stopped by Jean gently pulling her back.

Anna bit her lip and braced herself, "I'm sorry about your car Jean."

"Don't be daft hen. I got a new one off the insurance. The main thing is your looking after oor Claire."

"I am. Well we look after each other."

Jean pulled her further back from the door and lowered her voice,

"I don't know what went on that night, but I know that she's happy now, living with you and doing something with her life. Just, please, let me know if she's struggling. Will you?"

Anna nodded, Jean continued, without a break.

"Look hen, I didnae know if I should tell you about your dad or not. So I told Claire, and she decided we should."

"You did the right thing. He's obviously looking for me. Where did you see him?"

"I dropped the bairns off at school this morning, and I had to go down the High Street. I was driving down the hill past Christine's, and there he was. I was like, no way is that Anna's old man? I couldn't believe ma eyes, so I did a u-turn, at the bottom of the hill, it is definitely him. I drove back up and looked right at him. You couldnae mistake that face. It's been a while, but I never forget a face..."

Anna knew Jean would keep talking till something stopped her, so she interrupted, "He must be at Christine's! I'm going there now."

"It's too late, hen, it's after midnight. Get a good night's sleep here and find him first thing in the morning. That's your best bet, if you go knocking on folk's door at this time..."

"I can't wait. What if he leaves? What if I can't find him?"

Jean placed a hand on each of Anna's shoulders, "Look, we don't know for sure he's there. You're not wandering the streets in the dark on your own. Just calm down. I'll make a bed up, and tomorrow you can find him. Right, now, tea? Toast? Come through, come on."

Anna took a big breath in and dropped her rucksack at her feet. She was pretty hungry, and she could do with some sleep first.

After the boys calmed down, bellies were full, and everyone was ready to sleep, Jean directed them up to Claire's old room. Not much evidence of her time there remained—only the navy blue sun, moon, and stars curtains. Jean had set up the sofa cushions into a bed shape on the floor, topped with a red nylon sleeping bag.

As Anna listened to Claire brush her teeth in the bathroom, she stripped down to her knickers and wriggled inside her bed for the night. The rough edges of her toenails caught on the inside lining.

Claire returned in a nice cotton nighty and placed her clothes in a neat pile on the desk. She stepped over Anna's crumpled jeans and jumped into her old bed.

"It's good to be back, just for a little while," Claire said quietly as she breathed in the scent of Lenor from the pillowcase. "Are you nervous about seeing your dad?"

Anna had slipped between the sofa cushion already; her bum was on the floor.

"Yes. So much. Half of me wants to cuddle him, and half wants to punch him in the face."

"What are you going to say to him?"

"I don't know, I've practiced it for years. All the questions, all the stuff I want to blame him for, all the stuff he missed out on. But now I might actually get the chance to say any of it; I've no idea what I'll do."

"I know what you mean. There's so much I want to say to my mum, but any time I've been to see her in the hospital, I can't bring myself to say anything."

CHAPTER TWO

2

Jackson

DI Jackson polished her nameplate; she folded the yellow duster and buffed in circular motions. As she placed it at just the right angle, a weak knock came, followed by a high-pitched squeak of the door hinge.

"Morning Jamie. Take note, please - buy wd40 for that bloody door, it's really starting to annoy me."

"Uh hu, will add that to my list. If you'd like me to shove a broom up my arse, I could sweep your floor while I'm doing it?"

"Don't be so crude. Things need to be maintained round here, and it's not like the janitor pays attention."

"Are you in one of your moods today?" Jamie sat on the corner of her desk, facing the framed newspaper cutting of the headline 'Project Brown Owl hailed success.'

She didn't reply, it was too easy to get into an argument with him, but it never ended with any satisfaction. Instead, she pretended he wasn't there. She placed the duster in the bottom drawer and reshuffled the blue and black pens into separate parts of the desk organiser.

He swung one knee over the other and leaned back on one hand.

"I know what your problem is. You're bored."

He was right. After the court case was tied up, there hadn't been anything to really get her teeth into. The Scouse gang had been stopped in their tracks. The junkies were living relatively quietly, and she'd found it was sometimes better to turn a bit of a blind eye to that, as long as they were keeping to their own kind and not bothering normal people. The gypsies were still up to all sorts, of course, and she would eventually bring them down, but she wasn't really looking forward to that. Gypsy business was complicated and very hard to get anything to go on. She'd seen the mess Walker made turning up to the camp with warrants in the names of people that didn't even exist. Bar fights and domestics were too petty for anyone to get any decent kudos, and traffic offenses were so far beneath her these days.

"Here's something to cheer you up. The Christmas party! I'm organising it again this year, since everyone said I did a wonderful job last time. I just need to know what your clothes size is..."

"I'm not getting dressed up. You're not buying me anything to wear. No tinsel, no Santa hats."

Jamie was visibly hurt. "My god, you are a miserable woman. No wonder you're single!"

Jackson felt the rage bubble in her gut. She stood up and pushed her spinning chair away; she pointed inches from Jamie's face. "I don't know who the hell you think you're talking to, but I'm..."

As Jamie leaned away from her telling off, the phone rang. He slipped off the side of the table.

"You better answer that, since you're so important!" He ran out of the door and slammed it like a dramatic teenager.

Jackson regained her composure and picked up the receiver.

"Hello, North East division, DI Jackson speaking, how can I help you." She caught sight of the lines between her eyebrows in her reflection and smoothed them out with her fingers. An English accent. Interesting.

As the call progressed, she felt an exciting twinge in her belly. She took notes;

Swindon constabulary.
Contact: Paul Fowler
Organised crime Surveillance unit.
One way tickets up here!
2 men,
Frankie De'Coza, bald, 5.10
Billy McHail, stocky, 5.8, blond short back and sides.
Firearms!!
What are they doing here??
Keep watch till Swindon team get here.

"Ok, I've got all the details. Leave it with me. I'll be in touch as soon as I get a sighting." As she replaced the receiver, she punched the air.

"Yes, yes, yes!!" realising where she was,

she put a hand over her mouth and sat quietly, hoping she hadn't attracted any attention.

This was far too good to share. She would watch these guys. She'd do whatever it took to catch them up to something and take them out before the Swindon team made it up here.

Their train was due at the station in 4 hours; she needed the unmarked car and a wingman.

Claire

"There's a light on at Christine's, oh god, what if he's not here?" Anna said as they pulled up in Jean's car just before 10 am.

"Just go and knock on the door," Claire replied.

"What if he tells me to go away? Or maybe he won't even recognise me. No, let's just go home. This was a stupid idea."

"Come on, just get it over with. Yesterday you didn't even know if he was dead or alive, now you're here, and the only thing you can do is go and knock on that door."

"What if it wasn't even him? Maybe Jean was mistaken?"

"If it wasn't him, then just tell Christine you're visiting her, and then we'll go, but you've got to find out."

"Will you come?"

"I can't, I don't want to get caught out by anyone. I'm going to sit here, with the car running and the doors locked, ok?"

"Chill out, no one's going to see us here."

"I'm not taking the risk. Just give me a thumbs up if he's there, or a wave if it's just Christine."

"Right, I'm just going to do it. What's the worst that could happen? He rejects me, and I'm forced to live with Daddy issues the rest of my life?" Anna opened the door and swung her left leg out of the car, then turned back to Claire, and with a laugh said,

"Oh, wait!"

Claire laughed too, and shook her head. She could easily be weighed down by her thoughts of the father she never met, but Anna's 'Daddy issues' jokes always kept things light.

As Anna bounced up the pavement, in a cloud of her own breath in the icy morning air, Claire locked the car doors, pulled her hood up around her face, and sunk back into the seat. She couldn't believe she was sitting in this town again, breaking every promise she'd made to herself over the last six months. She looked in each mirror in turn, feeling her anxiety rise. It didn't matter how often Anna assured her that no one knew. It didn't make a difference how often she repeated it to herself; the truth that she had killed Shaun in her house that night haunted her every day.

Bazz had pleaded guilty to manslaughter, and his time was reduced, with self-defense as mitigating circumstances. Anna kept telling her how much Bazz thought they had done him a favour. She knew it wasn't a favour; the guilt of taking advantage of him had kept her awake every night since.

She replayed it daily, multiple times. The weight of the iron, the carpet beneath her knees, her tear stained, wet collar becoming colder round her neck. The smell of warm blood. Sometimes she'd see the outline of his still body on the floor, in the darkness of her room at night. Sometimes she'd catch a glimpse of his face in a crowd or on the bus to work. It had been getting easier, when the thoughts came now, she would start making a list of colours she could see or thinking of items in her kitchen. But now, being back here, it was becoming harder and harder. She was too close. Too much reminded her of that night.

She watched Anna knock for the third time, turning back to the car with a desperate look. From where Claire sat, she'd seen the blinds twitch at the first knock. Then a curtain upstairs briefly parted. She prayed Anna hadn't noticed and didn't know she was being ignored.

Claire wanted to go and drag her away, drive them as far away from this horrible place as possible. Her heart was breaking for her friend.

Anna visibly deflated. With shoulders drooped, she reached for the gate. Then she turned back, towards the house again, the door was opening, Claire could see Christine's familiar shape, arms welcoming Anna inside.

Claire watched for the wave or thumbs up, but Anna gave neither. The door closed on the once so familiar house, on the once so homely street. She thought back to the hours the pair hand spent sitting on that wall, in ponytails and leggings, planning their future as adults. None of this was ever part of it.

Anna

"Is my dad here?"

"Come in and sit down," Christine said with open arms.

"I don't want to sit down, just tell me, is it true? Is he here?"

Anna pushed past her into the living room. She stopped, frozen to the spot. Her body wouldn't take her any further.

There he was. Older, of course, his hair still dark but thinning on the top. He sat relaxed with one foot resting on his knee, like it was the most natural thing in the world, not to have seen your daughter for almost a decade. Christine gently tapped her shoulder, "I'll give you some privacy. Just shout if you need me, ok?"

No words came. Anna felt a lump begin to form in her throat. He slowly stood, still in silence; he spread his arms and tilted his head softly.

"Anna, my girl. I've missed you."

Her body refused to move. Her mouth was uncooperative. Inside, a million thoughts fought for acknowledgment, but none could take hold.

He went to her; she was taller by a couple of inches. He wrapped his arms around her, placing his head on her tense shoulder.

As he squeezed, she tensed more, and then she pushed him away.

"Where the hell have you been?" She felt the anger move the skin around her eyes into harsh lines.

"It's hard to explain. Things have been complicated."

"You don't say? Do you think it wasn't complicated for me when my mum died? You think it wasn't complicated having no fucking parents?" Her voice rose, and she felt acid in each word.

"I'm so sorry about your mum, I wanted to come back when I heard, but things happened. It was out of my control."

"You knew she was dead, and I was alone. Your only daughter, alone. You couldn't even get on a train and come and see me." Her jaw tightened, and the words whistled between her teeth.

He held both her hands and looked her straight on. Her eyes were filling, she couldn't see, her bottom lip trembled.

"I'm sorry my darling. I'm here now. I

know, I've got a lot of making up to do." He pulled her close again; this time she didn't tense, her body gave in, she broke down in huge sobs, her arms moved from her sides. Hesitantly, she hugged him back. He still had the same scent, Brut mixed with Benson and Hedges, the same smell as the last hug on her 10th birthday.

She felt the pain of all the other missed birthdays, and she wanted to push him away. But her heart stopped her. She allowed the moment to grow. She accepted his affection, then a wave of cold as she remembered the empty years, and she pulled back from him.

He sat down and patted the sofa next to him while taking the same relaxed posture again. Anna declined and perched on the edge of the footstool, ready to leave if she decided to. Using her hand to steady her, she felt crumbs on the velveteen and brushed them onto the floor.

"So tell me, how's life in Ibiza? You must be freezing coming back here." He asked. Anna studied his eyes as he spoke. She'd forgotten they were the same shade of hazel as her own.

"Oh no, I didn't go. Things changed things out of my control. You know how that goes." She dried her eyes with her sleeve. "Where do you live anyway? Your accent's changed."

"Ah, I've been around a few places, nowhere very permanent. I had to develop this generic sound so people could understand me. Do I sound daft?"

"A bit." She cracked a smile. "How long are you staying for?"

"Well, it was just a flying visit to see you, then I heard you were out of the country, so I was heading off. But now you're here, I guess things have changed."

"I can't hang around long, my friend's waiting in the car outside. We're not staying in town. Some things happened before I left, you know, things out of my control. So I can't stay long." She knew there was an edge to her tone; she wanted him to hear her repeat his excuse and see how it felt.

"I want to get to know you again. We need more time, there are things we need to talk about."

"Like what? Just tell me now. I've got to go."

"Will you come back? Later on? Surely

you can spare me a little longer?"

"Well, I could, maybe come for a while later. I'd need to sort it out with my friend."

"Let's eat together tonight—just us. I'll sort it out with Christine. We can build some bridges and figure out where to go from here. What do you say?"

"Yeah, ok."

"Do you still like fish fingers and peas?"

"Dad, I'm nearly 20. Yes, I do. With salad cream."

"I remember. I'll have it ready. Come about 6."

He didn't get up, just remained relaxed on the sofa and raised an easy little wave as she got ready to leave.

"Six o'clock then. See you here, yeah?"

He nodded.

She couldn't leave Claire sitting outside any longer, so she shouted, "I'll catch up with you later, Christine! I've got to go."

She bounced back down the steps and towards the steamed-up car. She knocked on the passenger window and gave Claire the thumbs up.

Claire

Claire was happy to listen to Anna's mixed emotions, she could hear the excitement in her voice overtaking the anger, and it was taking her out of her own head. As she drove back towards her auntie's, Anna wound the window down, lit a cigarette, and said,

"Now that's out the road, we've got something important to do. We need to visit Bazz."

Claire felt her heart beating in her ears. Sweat trickled between her breasts. She had to wipe her hands on her coat to stop them from slipping on the steering wheel.

"I can't. No way. I can't go in there. What if they know. Someone might know what I did." The car scraped on the kerb, and bounced back out into the road. She pushed her hood off to let some heat out. They swerved over the white line. A horn blasted from behind them.

"Pull over. Just stop the car now."

"Not here, what if someone sees us!" Claire hands were shaking on the wheel.

"Just stop here! Pull over!"

Claire slammed the brakes on; the car behind blasted the horn as it swerved past them. Anna pulled the hand brake and shifted the stick to neutral. She threw the cigarette out and wound the window up in case anyone heard.

"Listen to me. No one knows what happened. Only me, you, and Bazz. No one else. You've done nothing wrong. You saved my life. He was going to kill me, and you stopped him."

Claire's entire body was shaking.

"You don't need to come in, ok? Just drop me off. Wait in the car park for me; then we'll go back to your aunties and stay inside. You've done your bit. I'm sorry I made you come, but I just need this little bit of help today, ok?"

"Ok, then can we go home?"

"Soon, there's one more thing. I need to see my dad tonight, and then we will get the train out of here first thing tomorrow."

"Another night? Are you serious? I can't deal with this. I'm a nervous wreck."

"You don't need to do anything else; after this, you can chill out with Jean, enjoy seeing the wee boys, and we'll be ready to go home before you know it."

Christine

"Get away from that window!" Christine whispered.

"Why did I have to hide up here? This is stupid."

"He just wants it to be the right time to tell her. It's a big thing meeting your dad after all these years. Never mind finding out you've got wee sister you never knew existed."

"Do you think she'll like me?" The little girl asked as she sat on the edge of the neatly made bed.

"Course she will. She's never had a sister. What's no to like?"

"Was she like me when she was little?" her fingers were pulling at the gathered lace edging of a decorative pillow.

"She was quite cheeky. Are you cheeky?" Christine nudged her with her elbow, she giggled, and Christine whispered,

"Sssshhh!"

She pulled a thread from the edge of the lace; it grew between her fingers.

"Sometimes, I do get in a lot of trouble. From my mum, she was always shouting at me."

"So, where is your mum then?"

"Erm, I don't really know. Sometimes things are just for adults to know."

"That's right, I suppose."

She stared at the wall, and with a gentle tug, unraveled an inch of lace. She looked up at Christine with a face that said, 'I really didn't mean to do that.' Christine would have usually reprimanded Anna for picking and wrecking her stuff, but against every instinct, she ignored it.

"Dad says sometimes the adults need to sort things out before the kids need to know what's going on."

"Does he indeed? Well, let's hope he's got things sorted with Anna so you can meet her." Christine's eyes kept flitting back to the lace that was now billowing from the edge of the silky cushion, the multiple threads dangling from the exposed rough edge. She wanted to grab it, but she wouldn't.

"What kind of pizza is her favourite." The little girl asked.

"I'm not sure. Just cheese, I think." Christine slid her hands under her thighs to stop her from reaching out to save the cushion.

"Wow, that's actually my favourite too."

Her little eyebrows raised, "what's her favourite animal?"

"I've no idea pal. You'll be able to ask her all these things soon."

"Well, I hope she likes dolphins. They're my favourite. Do you think she does like dolphins?"

Christine moved over to the door, partly to get away from the sacrificed lace, but mostly to try and hear what Anna just shouted from the hallway.

"Ssshh"

The little girl covers her mouth and tries to hold her breath. Her cheeks puffed out and reddening by the second. As the front door closes, Christine watches Anna bounce down the steps, onto the road, and into a red car.

"Come on, let's go down," Christine said.

The girl jumps off the bed, gasping for breath.

"Right now?" the little girl tenses with excitement, then runs down the stair at a rate that makes Christine nervous.

"Careful," she shouts from behind.

Andy sat, one foot rested on the other knee, smiling as she burst into the living room looking around for another face.

"Where is she?"

"She had to go."

The little girl held her hands out, waiting for more information. Andy gave her none.

"Well, what did she say? When's she coming back?"

"Look, baby girl, it's complicated. I just..."

She folded her arms across her chest. "Why is everything always complicated?"

"Come and sit here." He patted the sofa next to him.

"No. Just tell me. Does she not want to meet me?" She remained stubbornly in the same position.

"Well, I didn't exactly tell her yet."

"Dad! Why not? Don't you think it's important?"

"Come on, sit here." He slides up a little, patting the seat again.

"No. You said you'd tell her as soon as we found her."

"Don't get upset. I wanted to do it at the right time. It's very special news, and I want to tell her at a special moment."

She sighed and reluctantly dropped onto the sofa.

Christine narrowed her eyes at Andy.

He silently mouthed, "what?"

Christine subtly shook her head. "I'm putting on a pan of soup. It will be ready for lunch. Why don't you come and give me a hand peeling the carrots." She went to the kitchen, leaving father and daughter alone.

Andy

"You do want to tell her, don't you?" Alice said.

"Of course I do. It's why we came here."

"What about the other thing?"

"Shhhh." He put his finger to her mouth. She backed away from his hand.

"When are we doing it?" she whispered.

"Tonight. It has to be tonight. It's our only chance."

CHAPTER THREE

3

Anna

The uniformed officer ran a finger down the list of names, shaking his head.

"I'm definitely on the list. It's Anna, with an A."

The middle-aged man with salt and pepper hair looked over the top of his glasses without lifting his head.

"And here was me looking for Anna with a J." He flicked the page and again, running his finger down the paper.

"Ah, Anna, with an A, here you go. Take a seat in the waiting room, and you'll be called for a search once we are ready for you."

She took a seat on a molded red plastic chair. The floor was grey lino. The walls painted magnolia. The desk staff watched through the triple-glazed window. The only decoration was information posters, Samaritans, child-line, Alcoholics Anonymous, and victims of crime support.

Opposite, a woman with 2-inch brown roots and yellow bleached hair bit the skin off the sides of her nails. The lines around her mouth made Anna consider stopping smoking for a minute.

In the corner, wearing a navy Adidas tracksuit, a 20 something reclined with his arms folded across his chest, legs stretched out in front, taking up the walkway. His body language said he didn't give a shit. But the sweat drops over his top lip told a different story.

Anna didn't want to attract any conversations by catching anyone's eye, so she got engrossed in picking the dirt from beneath her nails. They were all perfectly white by the time the heavy door opened, and a scary looking woman beckoned her inside.

The small room was horribly bright, with a bare fluorescent strip above. There were no windows and no furniture: only a fitted worktop, a box of latex gloves, and a little lined bin in the corner.

She started to cringe when calculating how long she'd had these knickers on for. She wasn't feeling very fresh. Certainly not fresh enough for a stranger to be poking about. Anna gulped, feeling the blood rise up her neck and face. She started with the top button of her jeans.

"Hold on." The woman smiled and held a hand up. "Just empty your pockets, then stand with your legs apart. You don't need to strip."

Anna was relieved and embarrassed. She decided to just follow instructions and not act on her initiative in here; she didn't have a clue what she was doing.

She was patted down, turned around, her shoes inspected, jacket emptied, ears, hair, and mouth checked.

"Ok, that's you, all clear, and no one had to get naked." The woman pushed the second door open, and Anna tentatively made her way into the visiting room.

She scanned the low chairs and tables, but she couldn't pick out her friend. The room looked like it was full of grown-ups sitting at nursery furniture. Over the hum of quiet conversations, she heard him from the left. His arm stretched up over the rest.

A white-toothed smile, over broad shoulders. Bazz was almost unrecognizable.

"Anna, so good to get a visitor, man. I thought you was never coming."

"I'm sorry, I was nervous about coming back up here, you know, with folk still looking for me." She took the seat, and the table touched her shins, too low to pass anything underneath. She leaned over to hug her friend but was halted with a sharp whistle. She withdrew to her side of the table.

"You look amazing. So healthy."

"I got me teeth fixed. And, check these out..." he lifted his arm and tensed to show his bicep was twice the size of the skinny version of Bazz she'd last seen on TV in the back of the police car.

"Impressive." She gave an affirming nod, "But, how are you really? Is there anything I can do? After what you've done for Claire and me, I..."

"Are you kidding? Look at us! I love it in here. Everyone thinks I'm someone. I've become someone. I've never mentioned a single name. So everyone thinks I'm loyal and solid." He leans in slightly, lowering his voice to barely audible. "It's easy in here. They don't have a clue, I don't drop names coz I don't know any! I'm a killer, with unknown connections. I keep myself to myself, go to the gym and eat three meals a day." He beamed, with more certainty than she'd ever seen him with.

"I'm so glad, we've been thinking about you all the time, about how grateful we are, about the sacrifice you made for us. We just want to pay you back somehow."

"There is one thing."

"Of course, anything."

"Have yous still got any money left?"

"Yeah, plenty. Well, I'd say plenty. Claire says we need to be sensible with it, but there's some left, yeah. What do you need?"

"Not for me, I've got everything I need. It's Wendy. Can you go and give her some money?"

"Wendy Monroe? Are you in touch with her?"

"She writes us letter sometimes. She's waiting for us. We're going to be together."

"Aw, wow, that's great." Anna bit her lip, "I'm really happy that's working out for you both. She's such a, er, she's really, um, you know, nice. She's a nice girl."

"She's the best thing that's ever happened to us. I read every letter she sends a hundred times. She sprays Charlie Red on the envelope, I close my eyes, and I can smell her. It reminds me of working in the community service van and the laughs we had."

Anna was relieved to see how content her hapless friend was.

"That's lovely, how romantic."

"The only thing is, she thinks I'm, you know, connected. That I've got money."

"Right, so she's waiting for you, and you're all loved up, but she needs some of your gangster cash while she's waiting?"

Bazz nodded enthusiastically.

"So, can you go and give her some? A couple of hundred should do it."

"Mate, it's the least I can do. I'm trying to stay under the radar while I'm up here, but I will do that for you."

They chatted some more, about jail food, and hierarchy, Anna's high life in the city and the low life back home, then she promised to write and to visit again soon.

A long whistle signaled the end, a brief

hug was allowed. She held him tight and squeezed, and he squeezed back.

"I'll tell Wendy you are looking good, ok?"

Bazz stood tall as she walked back out the guarded doors.

She counted seven locked doorways to the outside world. She squinted at the bright light, pulled her jacket tight across her chest, and walked briskly in the direction of Jean's car.

She decided not to mention the donation they were about to make to Wendy Monroe. Claire wouldn't grudge Bazz anything; she owed him her freedom, but scouring the town for a strung-out junkie when they were supposed to be in and out with no drama, might stress her out a bit.

Anna

"Bazz is happy. I swear, I told him you appreciate everything he's done."

"He can't be happy. He's in jail, for at least the next four years."

"You remember what he was like don't you? He was hopeless, jobless, and toothless. Now he's a new man. He feels like he's really made something of himself and that he's finally done an honorable thing."

"I feel so guilty I didn't come in. I just couldn't."

"It's ok, stop torturing yourself. No one is blaming you, ok. We need to get past this somehow."

"That's easy for you to say. You didn't cave someone's skull in."

"Neither did you. You were saving my life! There's only so many times we can go over all this."

"Don't get annoyed with me. Coming back here, it's made it all worse. I thought I could forget, but everything reminds me."

"I'm sorry I made you come. Look, go back to Jean's, and stay indoors. I've got to see my dad. Then I'll be straight back tonight."

"You can't walk around this place as if nothing happened; someone will see you! You're crazy, I'm not letting you."

"Ok, ok, calm down. I'm not planning on it. I'll do what I need to and nothing else, no risks, no bumping into anyone. Stop worrying. Drop me here, and I'll get you back at Jean's later."

Claire looked ill. Her shaking hands slipped around the steering wheel.

"Look, I'll keep my hood right up. I won't stop for anyone. You go and lock the door when you get in."

Claire pulled in at the train station, and Anna jumped out. With her hood up and her hands tucked in her pockets, she could have been anyone.

With Claire safely away, she could get on with the rest of the business she needed to attend to.

1, find Wendy Munroe

2, find out how much trouble she was really in. For the last six months, she'd imagined getting hunted down by Archie, Davie, and Ronin, all fighting each other to be the one to wring her neck. She needed to know where she stood.

There was only one person who was likely to have all this information.

The Nags Head had always been a favourite place in the winter; it was cozy and festive. She'd loved sipping on vodka, looking out at the frosty street. Today she felt like she was walking to the guillotine.

She pushed the door open a little, trying to see as much as possible. On the right sat a couple of old ladies with shopping bags and tiny glasses of sherry. On the left, a man in a pink sweater with a golden lab eating cheese and onion crisps from an open bag on the floor. And polishing the brass taps behind the bar was Gemma.

She pushed the door a little further; the warmth and smell of old beer and smoke were welcoming. Once she was sure there was no one else lurking inside, she stepped in, removed her hood, and hopped onto the velvet bar stool.

"Well, well, look who it isnae. You've not got much of a tan, have you?" Gemma looked her up and down.

"How's it going?" Anna gave her the customary fake smile.

"Aye, you see it all, same shit different day. When did you get back?"

"Em, just now, can I have a vodka and coke, please?"

"Where's your Davie? Is he back as well?"

"Davie? Oh, no. Not this time." Anna realised she was supposed to have made it to Ibiza, this was a good start.

"What about Archie?"

Anna's toes curled inside her shoes, she dug her nails into her palms.

"What about him?"

"Is he back with you?"

"With me?" Anna tried to remain unreadable; inside she was terrified.

"Back from Ibiza, or is he staying with Davie. Are you just back for Christmas yourself?"

"Oh, right, yeah. I'm just back for a few days. Myself."

"Jesus Christ, you haven't changed, have you? You're so thick sometimes." Gemma threw too much ice into the glass.

"When I heard he hadn't been seen since you left, I thought you had maybe had a wee thing, but then I figured out yous all went to Ibiza together." Gemma pulled the trigger on the coke dispenser too hard, it foamed over the top onto the beer mat. Anna laughed.

"You thought me and Archie were having an affair, and we'd run away together? That's Hilarious."

"I just put two and two together, but then when Davie didn't phone again, I figured out you were all there together."

Anna wanted to freeze time, prize the

information out. What did she just say? Davie had phoned? He had been looking for her. But she couldn't ask, she couldn't even acknowledge what Gemma had said.

"You're so funny, wait till I tell them when I get back."

"I have to say; you proved me wrong."

"How's that?" Anna asked, wishing she wasn't there and taking the first fizzy sip of her drink.

"I thought you were no good for Davie. Though he'd be back here soon enough and get back with my sister, but you've stuck it out." Gemma buffed up the brass tap between them, and blew the bottom of her pristine fringe up out of her eyes. "She was broken-hearted when they finished, you know, but she's moved on now, got some someone way better. No offense."

"None taken," Anna wanted to laugh, to say her sister was welcome to the piece of shit, but she had a front to keep up.

"So, what's it like out there? Have you got a job? You must have money if you're still there." She blew the other side of her fringe out of the way.

"It's great, really nice."

"Are the pubs busy? Do you go out to the

big clubs? What about Archie? Is he seeing anyone?"

"It's all good, everyone's happy. I think he's into a nice Spanish woman just now, actually."

"Really? Where do you guys work?"

"Just in a bar. Anyway, what's been happening here? Any gossip?"

"Things have pretty quiet since that Bazz went to jail. Cannae believe it, a murderer, in this town! Now it's just the usual junkies having a carry-on up by mine but nothing too wild. It's kind of boring actually."

"Is Wendy Monroe still kicking about?"

"Ew yuck. I see her all the time, absolute waste of space. She's in and out of the cells every week. God knows how she's not in Courtonvale."

"She's still on the gear then?" Anna knew she'd get the information without even asking, she just needed to scratch the surface, and Gemma would fill the cracks in.

"Course she is. That will be the death of her. Waste of skin she is. Same with all the rest of them up at that flat."

"Where's that?"

"The snake pit. Or whatever you call it. Absolute shit hole full of reprobates."

"Ah, the viper room. I should have guessed."

Walking on those sticky floorboards into that rat trap was the last thing she wanted to do, but she promised Bazz.

"Gemma, can I have a double, please?"

"A double? At lunchtime? What's up with you like?"

"Nothing. I'm just glad to be here. It's just nice to see you." Anna's smile was as fake as Gemma's concern.

Gemma served another customer at the bar, leaving Anna in peace to take in the surroundings. This place was so familiar. The smells and sounds were the same, the layout remained as it always was, but something was different. She relished the warming glow while sipping the double a bit too quickly and guessed that it was her that was different. As she thought of all the new pubs and coffee shops she'd tried in Edinburgh, Gemma shouted,

"That reminds me, someone's looking for you! Someone you owe money to!"

Anna cringed and disguised it with a laugh as everyone looked her way.

"He's not a happy bunny." Gemma

pointed across the bar with a duster hanging from her hand.

"Who's that then?" Anna's head said 'run,' but her legs felt weak.

"Don't you even remember who your due money to?"

Anna downed the remainder of the glass and crunched on a bit of ice. She shrugged, extra casually.

"Can't think of anyone." She didn't make eye contact. She stared into the swirling ice as she circled the glass in her hand.

"Patrick, the guy you and Davie rented the flat off. Says you owe him rent and the price of getting the place cleaned up."

Anna heard tutting coming from the sherry drinkers. She felt her cheeks tingle.

"That's Davies department. I'll be sure to pass on the message." The mild embarrassment was washed away by relief. A disgruntled landlord wasn't likely to get violent, so he was the least of her worries.

She drained the very last of the meltwater from her glass, and hopped off the stool.

"Well Gemma, it's been lovely seeing you. Enjoy the cold, wet winter. Gotta go." She bared her teeth in a smile so insincere she felt horrible. Gemma returned a similar

look, but hers had an added edge,
"Safe journey."

As the vodka dulled her nerves and the caffeine and sugar boosted her energy, she felt a confusing mix of carefree-excitement. She bounced through the streets, eager to see people but wary still. She loved seeing her old hometown, noticing new things, and finding comfort in the parts that had never changed. But, she still had to be on her guard.

Gemma's concoction of facts and tainted observations were certainly not what Anna expected to hear. She was prepared to listen to warnings. She'd expected Archie to be after her blood, and furious Davie to be looking for revenge. She certainly didn't expect to hear that they were all living happily ever after in the sun.

This worryingly meant that either of them could turn up at any time. She would cross that bridge if she came to it. Neither of them was very bright, and the vodka helped her to calculate that it was practically impossible for them to turn up in town the same day she did.

The old landlord was small potatoes. He was at the bottom of the list.

More pressingly was Ronin and his extended Neanderthal family. She didn't even know half of them. Anyone could pass on a message to him that she was in town. The last she'd seen of him, he was on his knees holding his ripped-up arm on a garage forecourt. Goosebumps prickled her arms as she recalled the smell of petrol and the lights glinting on glass shards covering her body.

Yeah, he was her main problem. The reason she'd promised not to walk about the town, the reason she couldn't tell Claire about going to find Wendy, and the reason she definitely shouldn't have been in the Nags Head.

She pulled her hood up, and put her head down. She walked, almost skipping, in the directing of the Viper Room, hoping she wasn't making a huge mistake.

Jackson

"Jamie, I need your help." Jackson leaned over the reception desk and whispered.

"Oh, you need me now, do you? Well, I'm

not in the mood to get shouted at like a child." He folded his arms.

"You were right, I need cheering up, and you can help me. If you get me the keys for the unmarked car, I'll increase the Christmas party budget by fifty pounds."

"Oh my goodness, will you really? I'll make a fruit punch! And buy quality crackers, not the crap ones with the hats that just rip!"

"Shh, only if you keep it a secret and come with me?"

"Thought you said you'd never take me out with you again? Thought I was the most annoying person you've ever had the misfortune of working with?"

"Aw, don't be silly. I was just kidding. There's no one else I'd ask for such a top-secret job."

"Hmm, ok then. But, you have to wear a Christmas jumper."

"Ok, it's a deal. Now, go and get the keys and make your excuses. Do not tell anyone what we are doing, ok?"

Jackson put six sugars into her tea flask, filled her pockets with mini packets of digestives and ginger nuts. She remembered

Jamie was more palatable if there were snacks on hand. She took a new notebook from the storeroom. While waiting on the fire exit step for Jamie to come out with the keys, she folded the cover over and began to write.

'Project...'

She bit the end of the pen. She hadn't been allowed this project. In fact, she'd be in trouble if anyone found out she hadn't passed on the information from the call.

Project Wild Cat. That was perfect. A well-camouflaged, rarely spotted animal, an excellent hunter that makes light work of its prey. Plus, it sounded really cool.

When Jamie finally arrived with the keys, he was wrapped up like a carol singer in coordinating red hat, gloves, and perfectly hanging scarf.

"What? We are undercover, aren't we?"

"Yes, and you look great. Come on, let's just hope the battery's not run out since the cars been out of action that long."

The car started first time, the windows de-misted quickly, and the radio was tuned in nicely. This was going to be a successful mission; she could feel it.

They took position in the train station car park, the northbound exit in full view.

"So, tell me now, what are we actually doing on this secret mission?"

"We are watching people. A couple of dodgy characters from down south. A team from Swindon is on the way up, but they asked me to keep an eye on them till they get here."

"Uuuurrghh, surveillance? I hate surveillance. It's the most boring thing ever."

Jackson produced a three-pack of digestives and handed them to her companion.

"It's not for long. Have these and keep your eyes peeled for trains arriving."

The way he crunched the biscuits was affecting her blood pressure. She opened her flask and tested the temperature.

"So why are they even coming here?" A crumb hit her thigh. "I mean, what's so interesting about this place that English gangsters want to come here?"

Jackson drummed her fingers on the steering wheel. "That's what we want to find out, Jamie. This is the next big thing to get our teeth into. We stopped those scousers before they even got started. We can do it again."

"And why do we need to keep it a secret?"

"Because, it's better that way. Have you ever heard 'too many cooks spoil the broth?'"

"Yes. Have you ever heard 'Jackson just wants all the credit'?" he made woolly gloved air-quotes, and Jackson cringed. He was sometimes sharper than he looked.

"I don't get it. Are they bringing drugs?"

"I don't know yet. We'll watch who they get in contact with. We'll get some clues and hopefully catch them up to something before the others even get here."

"Do you really think that's a good idea? I mean, if it's part of a bigger operation… "

"Shh, here, have some more biscuits. Now let's be quiet while we watch."

Anna

She lifted her hand to knock, then looked at the door's surface. The black paint was scratched and chipped, revealing the rusty red undercoat. Big circular stamps dented the wood, paint flaked from the edges of the impression left by a dawn raid and a battering ram. There were kicks, scuffs, and some dried-up spit that had gone crusty before dribbling all the way down. It was green-tinged, with tiny popped bubbles, and the edges were curling. The outside letterbox was missing, so she knocked.

Coming from inside, she could hear the noise of people up to no good preparing to answer the door to someone they weren't sure of. Shouts turning to shushing, a back window slamming, something clattering in the hallway. Then the inside letterbox opened, and an unknown voice asked...

"Who is it?"

"Alright? How's it going?" Anna felt awkward, unsure if she should shout or whisper. Her question was met with silence.

"I'm looking for Wendy Monroe. Anyone seen her?"

"No, not seen her. Don't even know her." The letterbox snapped shut; Anna took a chance and poked her hand in to flip it back open.

"Look, I've got something for her. A present."

A finger from an unseen hand grazed her own inside the hole. She flinched, then leaned closer, but not too close, "It will be worth her while." She said it in a weird sing-song kind of voice that she might have used trying to bribe a small child. She cringed, and waited. She heard footsteps on bare floorboards, mumbled chatter, then lighter steps returning.

This time the unmistakable nasal drawl of Wendy.

"Who's looking for me? I've no done anything wrang."

"That you Wendy? It's Anna, Bazz's pal." She crouched on her heels, suddenly eye to eye with Wendy through the rectangular hole.

"I've got a message for you from Bazz."

Wendy wiped her nose with her sleeve and stood up. Anna heard the key turn. As the door opened, Anna could smell dirty old washing, mouldy cat food, and vomit. Wendy stuck her head out and looked up and down the street. Satisfied it was clear, and her visit wasn't a decoy for an ambush about to strike, she brought her in. Wendy led the way to the kitchen.

She couldn't tell if the dishes had ever been washed since the last time she was unfortunate enough to be in this rotten room. A new white fridge filled one of the dark cavities. Its brightness stood out like a neon sign in the grime of the neglected kitchen.

Wendy pulled her hair tight at the top of her head and retied the elastic bobble.

"So, what's the message? If he's wanting me to visit um, he'll need to give me money."

"I hear you're going to wait for him. That's nice. I'm glad. He's a good guy."

"Pft, a good guy? What use is that to anyone?" Anna could see the weariness in Wendy's eyes.

"I mean good to know. Good to have on your side."

"You think? I hear he's a big shot, but no really seen much evidence of that. Think he might be all talk."

"Are you kidding?" Anna fished the warm wad of cash from her pocket, "He's solid. He's loyal and trustworthy and well respected." Anna peeled each note off, dramatising the counting process. Wendy's eyes fixed on the growing pile of notes.

"There you go, £200. And there's plenty more where that came from if you do the right thing."

"Honestly? Is that all for me?"

"Yeah, he sends his love, and as long as he thinks you're waiting for him, you'll be kept sweet." Anna winked at Wendy, and she nodded back slowly and deliberately. Anna knew it would be spent by Wednesday, and Wendy would be doing anything she could for another payout. She also knew that Wendy was incapable of being faithful but hoped she understood what she had to do.

Wendy shuffled the notes from one hand to the other, counting it for herself; the kitchen door swung open, and Tina Dougherty burst in. She looked Anna up and down, narrowing her eyes,

"I didn't know you were back," she curled her lip to indicate her distaste.

Wendy stuffed her reward into her bra and zipped her cardigan up, glancing between the two.

"I'm not really, just a flying visit. I'm leaving town right now actually."

"Just a flying visit to dish out my cousin's cash, aye?" Tina glared pure poison at Anna as Maria joined her in the doorway.

Wendy took a step towards them both, her hands on her hips. "That's ma money, from ma man actually, and it's nuhin to dae we you."

"Look guys, nice to see you both, but I've got to go. I've got a ticket for the next train out of here. I've got a plane to catch." She stood a little taller and pushed past Maria attempting to fill the doorway, and she upped her speed towards the exit. She had the same feeling she did at 8, turning off the light and getting into bed before the monster underneath caught her foot. Everyone knew Tina liked to throw things, glasses, ashtrays, shoes. Anna struggled to turn the key as she expected a bang on the back of the head at any second. She tried turning it the other way, success!

Stepping out into the air was like coming up from the bottom of the sea. She slammed the door behind her and heard a muffled shout from inside,

"Aye, you better run!"

She walked as fast as she could without breaking into a sprint. As predicted, the Viper Room had been a terrible idea. Her work was done though, she could go and spend some time with her dad, stay undercover at Christine's, then her and Claire could go home to their proper life first thing in the morning.

Jackson

Jamie slept for two hours; she didn't wake him. She welcomed the sound of his bubbling throat instead of crunching or talking drivel. Another train stopped, then crawled up the line out of the station. The exit was clear. Maybe those tickets had been bought as a decoy. Perhaps they were never bound for her town after all. Perhaps someone was setting her up, testing her procedure following. An uneasy feeling crept up her neck.

No, it was true—there in the double doors of the platform.

Two men, one bald, one blond. Both in black wool coats, carrying duffel bags, looking like they just stepped into oz.

They looked around, located the solitary taxi in the rank. The bald one read from what looked like a yellow post-it note, the driver nodded, and they clumsily got in the back seat.

Jackson started the engine and elbowed Jamie. He spluttered with fright over the top of his woolly scarf. His eyes were puffy and his cheeks rosy.

"Look sharp, Jamie, they're here! We're following that taxi. Keep your wits about you."

"5 more minutes." He mumbled, closing his eyes again. Jackson hit the brake heaving him forward and snapping him into consciousness.

"Ugh, I'm so tired. It's too hot in here."

"Stop whining and pay attention."

They followed close behind the Volvo taxi. Through the town, across the back of the park, down by the library, across the bridge at the post office, up through the bad estate, and down past Roy's Spar.

"Where on earth are they going? I think they are onto us. He's trying to lose us. I'm going to hang back a bit." She let a car out of the junction between them, hoping they'd dismiss her following. The taxi drove around the bottom of the park, up past the graveyard, and onto the school at the top of the hill.

"Can you see his indicators, Jamie?"

"Hmm, not really, oh wait, they are turning left, go left, go left!"

The car between them carried on ahead, so she took it slow, keeping them just in her sight and no more. They were heading back down towards the town center. Finally, the taxi pulled into the side of the road, outside the Ashvale bed and breakfast. The wooden 'vacancies' sign swung squint on one hook. She slowed as she passed, trying to take in as much as possible without looking directly at them.

One handed money to the driver, the other dragged their duffel bags up to the door. Neither seemed to notice the silver Astra that had been following them.

Jackson rounded the end of the street and found herself facing the south platform of the train station. After turning back on herself, she reversed into a space, allowing a full view of the road. "What was all that about? Do you think they saw us?"

"Eh, no. It's pretty obvious what that was all about." Jamie said.

"What? They were trying to lose us, but they didn't even try to see our faces."

"They weren't trying to lose us, silly. The taxi driver wanted to make some money off a couple of out-of-towner's, so he took them a long way round."

Jackson felt like an idiot. She was out of practice, needed to switch her detective mode on.

"Shouldn't you call someone and update their position?" Every word from Jamie's mouth pumped her blood pressure up a notch.

"That's none of your concern. Just keep watch and be quiet."

Frankie

"A twin room? Is that what she booked? We come all this way, and we have to share a room." Billy moaned, scratching his blonde head.

"We've stayed in worse. Anyway, it won't be for long. As soon as we get what we came for, we're out of here." Frankie replied.

"How are we going to find them then? We can't exactly go knocking on doors, can we."

"He'll slip up, he always does, but this time we'll be ready. He's not getting away this time." Billy emptied his bag on the delicate floral patterned bedspread. In the middle landed a dirty, stained bundle of cloth. He pulled a corner and watched it unravel, its shiny black contents hit the bed with a thud.

"This time, I'll be waiting." He picked up the handgun and pointed it towards himself in the mirror.

"But I'll tell you one thing for nothing, I

ain't walking around this town looking for him. We need a motor, pronto."

Frankie unfolded the green newspaper from inside his long wool coat.

"Have a look at the classifieds. We can pick up a cheap banger for the next few days. And wrap that bloody thing up, we ain't having that old dear walking in here and phoning the cops." He pulled a creased suit from his bag, hung it from a hanger, tutted, and pulled out a shoe polishing kit. "The state of that. I need an iron."

Billy took a lace doily from the top of the bookcase, folded it, and used it to polish his fingerprints off the gun. Then he wrapped the entire thing in it and popped it under the pillow, encased in floral lace.

"Ere, what about this one." He pointed a sausage-like finger at a basic add with no photo,

"ford escort, five door, dark blue, mot and tax for three months, quick sale so low price."

"I'm not fussy, as long as I don't have to get rained on or blistered feet looking for him. Give it a phone." He threw the mobile phone and laughed at him fumbling to catch it.

As the taxi pulled up, the men looked at each other.

"I ain't buying a motor off these dodgy gypsies." Billy shook his head.

"Yes we are. We ain't got time to mess about. We need a car now, and they've got one."

"This is a bad idea," Billy gave the driver a tenner and didn't wait for change.

As they walked into the mouth of the caravan set up, they were greeted by Tina and Maria.

"Hiya, who you boys looking for?" Maria asked.

"Are you selling something?" Tina moved closer to them.

"We're buying, actually. The blue Escort from the advert in the paper. You know who's it is?"

Tina nodded, "Wait there with her, I'll get my cousin for ya." She ran off between two caravans.

"So, you aren't from around here, are you? Where you from?" Maria unzipped her coat and twirled her gold chain between her thumb and finger.

Billy licked his top lip. "Swindon darling, just passing through."

"Shut it you. We don't tell no one where we're from."

"Don't worry about this little sweetheart. You ain't telling no one, are you?"

Maria flicked her hair and shifted her weight to the hip nearest him. "Nope, don't worry about me."

Ronin appeared from between two caravans, marching through the mud in his wellies.

"You just phoned my ma? About the car?"

Both men nodded, Billy still had his eyes fixated on the skin of Maria's neck.

"This way, boys. Maria, you get back to your van. Your mother's looking for you."

They followed closely behind Ronin, trying to avoid the mud, past tied-up dogs, dirty kids, and angry-looking women.

They stood in a row, looking at the bubbling paintwork, bald tires, and cracked back window.

"Three hundred and fifty quid, right now,

and you can take it away." Ronin said, offering his hand out.

"Is it reliable?" Frankie asked.

"How reliable are you expecting for that price? You want a cheap car, here's a cheap car."

Frankie and Billy look at each other. Billy shrugs and looks over his shoulder, hoping to see where Maria went.

"Two fifty." Frankie offered his hand.

Ronin blew air from his nostrils. "Three hundred, best price."

"Deal." Frankie pulled a roll of notes from his deep in his side pocket and began peeling off fifties. "Have you got the documents?"

"No documents."

Frankie stopped counting and asked, "We ain't going to get pulled over by the police in this rust bucket, are we?"

"We don't want no heat." Added Billy.

"It's not a dodgy motor, trust me, boys."

Billy snorted an ugly laugh. "Trust you? I met you two minutes ago."

"Well, well, you'll have to take the chance then, won't you. I wouldn't do that to you boys. You're clearly not dafties."

"No, we ain't. You definitely do not want

to do that to us."

"Boys, you give me the cash. You take this car. It's not exactly a motor for life. But, something tells me you aren't in this for the long run. Am I right?"

"You are," Billy nodded, "we just need it to find.."

Frankie interrupted, "Shut it, you. The man doesn't need to know our business."

"Say no more boys. I'm good at keeping secrets. Got plenty of my own, if you know what I mean." Ronin prodded the side of his nose and winked.

"Here's the keys. If anyone asks who I sold it to, I'll not say a word."

"Likewise mate, I like how you do business." Frankie shook his hand. Both men got in the car, adjusted the seats and mirrors, and slowly drove past the onlooking array of kids and animals.

"Here, why don't we ask him if he knows where McVay might be?" Billy suggested.

"No chance, have you got a death wish? Buying this car off these gypsies went against every value I've got. I am not getting into bed with them for anything."

"And I ain't into hanging about this shit

hole any longer than necessary. He braked, then reversed, carefully passing the confused onlookers.

"I cannot fucking believe you're doing this." Frankie said, pinching the bridge of his nose as they reversed back to where they left.

Ronin stood with his hands on his hips, jaw jutting forward. "You got a problem?"

"Na mate, just a question. You don't by any chance know the whereabouts of a man going by the name of Andy McVay?"

"McVay? That certainly rings a bell. But I can't be sure."

"Is he a friend of yours?" Billy asked.

"Are you calling me a liar?"

"Na mate, he's just wondering if you've heard of him, that's all." Frankie leaned cross to diffuse the growing tension.

"If I was to come across him, who should I say was looking?"

"No, don't tell him anything! We are trying to catch him, not have a reunion."

Billy felt Frankie's elbow in his ribs as he hissed into his ear, "You are fucking priceless. Stop opening that big mouth of yours!"

"Don't worry about it mate, thanks for the

car. It was a pleasure doing business with you."

"The pleasure was all mine, fellows." Ronin replied.

Frankie wound the window up and sighed, "Get us out of here."

CHAPTER FOUR

4

Hillary

"Here's three hundred quid. I sold that old ford today, and the money's for you. Treat yourself, my darling." Ronin stood in front of Hillary and tossed the cash onto her lap. She folded the fifties and inserted them carefully into her leather purse while sat on the edge of the low bed.

"While you were making sweetie money, you'll never guess who turned up in town today?"

"Give me a break woman, I'm doing what I can. There's three hundred quid there, and I'm giving it all to you. Do you see me spending it? No, because you..."

"Oh, do stop wingeing. I'll make it worth your while tonight, yes?"

"Tonight?" he gently wrapped his fingers in her brushed out blond curls and tipped her head back. "How about now?" she could see he was hard; he pulled her face forward and pressed himself against her. She grabbed the back of each thigh, and opened her lips to feel the throbbing through his jeans. He pulled her hair a little tighter. She spread her open legs wider, pulling him closer as her breathing deepened. He tilted her head to look up at him.

"So, who's back in town?"

She ignored his question and moved her hands higher up his thighs. He gripped her hair tighter.

"Spit it out then."

"Anna McVay. Tina saw her earlier."

Ronin's jaw clenched, his teeth grinding together. "She's got the nerve to come back here? I will kill that robbing little bitch." He let go of her hair and pushed her away. She watched the bulge in his jeans deflate and wished she'd never mentioned the news, at least till she was finished. Frustration tied a knot in her stomach so tight she had to stop herself from kicking him.

"Apparently, she had some money too, from what Tina saw."

"My fucking money," he slammed his fist on the worktop, the caravan vibrated. She could see the tightness in his muscles, the veins pulsing on his forearms, and sinews in his neck. All that passionate energy, wasted while she sat still catching her breath. Her unused arousal was turning to bile in her stomach and churning into hatred.

"Personally, I'm still shocked that you even attempted to do business with that girl after what her father did to your family."

"What are you going on about, woman?"

"Quite an armature move."

"You better stop winding me up and tell me what you're talking about."

"Tina and Maria told me all about it. Her father had some terrible business with your grandfather before he died."

"Her father? What's his name?" Ronin was tugging his earlobe furiously.

"Andy McVay." Hillary laughed, "How didn't you know?"

He stamped his foot and punched the toilet door; it came off the hinges and fell on top of the chemical toilet.

"I didn't know they were related! How the

hell would I have known that?"

"Well, it's not exactly a common name, is it? You'd of thought it would set off some alarm bells, no?" Hillary was enjoying seeing the rage pour out of him. He was baring his teeth, and she wondered if he might even hit her. She laughed again, leaning back on the bed out of his reach, then he stopped. The rage subsided, and he stared at the wall. She looked at him, curious as to what was coming next. Was he going to cry? His face looked like he was doing a hard sum in his head, she laughed again.

"Shut your mouth, I'm thinking." He snapped, still looking at the wall.

"Oh how wonderful. What on earth will you come up with this time, I wonder?"

"He must be worth something to those fellows in the car. I know he's worth something to my family for sure."

"Who? What are you talking about?"

"The English boys that bought the escort, they were in town looking for Andy McVay, the name rang a bell, but I didn't know why. Now I do." He was rocking from one foot to the other, and the caravan swayed along.

"The name rang a bell?" Hillary raised her

eyebrows and smirked.

"Shut it. It was ages ago, and no one's mentioned that name in years. I didn't know it was the same person! Look, if we brought him in, we could benefit, I'm sure of it."

"What do you mean, like kidnap him? Hold him ransom?"

"I'm not sure yet, but something tells me he's valuable."

"In money terms? What do you mean?"

"Maybe in money, but definitely as leverage against a bigger caravan. I reckon if I supply the man that robbed our granddaddy, we could get swapped into the big corner one. And, get back at that Anna, watching her daddy get his teeth knocked out, might persuade her to come up with my cash."

"A caravan with a separate bedroom?"

"If I bring in the man that robbed Old James Dougherty of his life savings, I'll get respect around here. But we need to find him before those English fellows do."

"You think he's in trouble?"

"They didn't look like they wanted to take him out for a picnic if that's what you mean."

"I'm in. If finding this chap gets me out of

this tin box, I'll do whatever it takes."

"We need to find him first, and the way to him is through that wee bitch Anna."

Christine

"I'm putting on extra chips if Anna's coming. That girl's always hungry."

"I'm always hungry too. We are so alike." The little girl swung her legs under the breakfast bar picking the label off the tomato sauce bottle. Andy's eyes glaze over as he watches out the window.

"Are you waiting for someone?" Christine asked.

"No, no, just jogging my memory. Thinking of the old days."

"Here lassie, take a couple of biscuits, go through and find some cartoons to watch." Christine handed the barrel over, and the child jumped down. She shut the door behind her and began whispering.

"Shame you didn't jog your memory a few years ago when the bairn needed you."

"Give me a break, Chris, I've told you, it's not that simple."

"That's a cop-out. That girl of yours has been a lost soul since her mum went."

"She's lucky you were here." Andy pulled out the other chair and positioned himself, ready for whatever Christine had in store for him.

"Her mum's old neighbour's not exactly a substitute parent, but you're right, I have been here." She turned the tap on and squeezed soap into the sink. Bubbles began to rise as she turned to point at Andy.

"I've seen her a rock bottom, you know. Hopeless, with nowhere to go. Look at her now. I'm so proud of the progress she's made."

Andy's face twinged with regret.

"I don't want you wrecking that." Her whisper was becoming a scolding. "You've come back into her life now; you cannae just go disappearing again."

He leaned on his elbows and touched his fingertips together like a politician.

"I don't know what might happen in the future Chris, no one does, but I'm here now. That's all I can say."

"Very good. As non-committal as ever. What are you like?"

"My life is tricky. I've got a lot going on, a lot of commitments. I'm just doing the best I can."

"The best you can? Well, for those two lassies sake, I really want to believe that."

"Chris, there's something you could do to help me out, make it a bit easier."

"What? Let you stay in my house, cook for you and entertain your daughter? Or, what? Something else?"

"Come on, give me a break. I could really do with your support here instead of just giving me a hard time."

Christine sighed while scrubbing the orange tea ring from the inside of a mug.

"I'm sorry ok. I just don't want to see her wee heart broken again."

"I promise, I'm doing the best I can, Chris." He put his hand on his heart.

She nodded and took a seat. "What can I do then?"

"I was thinking, maybe you could give us some time alone tonight? Just the three of us?"

Christine rolled her eyes, "So I've to clear out of my own gaff?"

"I just think it might be easier, less pressure."

"I'm kidding pal, that's no problem. I'll go round to my friends for a few hours. Leave you to bond with your girls."

Hillary

"Girls, can you help us out with a little something?" Hillary waved out of the passenger window.

"Depends. What's in it for us?"

"Well, you'd be helping your family. That's good enough, isn't it?"

"Just tell us where to find Anna McVay. Where will she be?" Ronin shouted over the top of Hillary's head.

"How am I supposed to know that?" Tina leaned on the side of the van, sticking her tongue through a mouthful of pink gum, trying to make a bubble.

"Think then! Who does she know?" He bounced, impatient.

The bubble shriveled away and stuck to her bottom lip. She nodded towards Hilary, "you got any fags?"

"Oh, come on girls. You can have all the cigarettes you like if you help us find her. Today."

"Well, we could think better if we had a smoke, I reckon," Maria said.

"Oh, for goodness sake," Hillary chided as she rummaged around her bag. "Here, now think," she passed a twenty pack and a lighter to Tina, "Where do you think she could be?"

Ronin's brow furrowed in the middle, "What have you got them fags for?"

"Oh, do be quiet. That's not our concern right now."

Tina's face beamed with satisfaction, "I'll tell you where you'll find her..."

Maria interrupted to finish the sentence, "she'll be with that mad old woman she hangs about with..."

"With the short hair, lives up..." Tina continued

"Green st." Maria finished.

Ronin tugs his earlobe, "That's it! Why didn't I think of that?"

Tina and Maria exchange a glance.

"I know exactly where that is. Get in the van. None of you girls mention this to anyone. This is my business, and you don't tell a soul, ok? Get in!"

"We're not coming, there's no room," Tina said, followed by a nudge from Maria. "I'll come. I could do with getting out of here for a while." She jumped in, and Hillary slid into the middle.

Ronin punched the steering wheel in

excitement.

The three females all looked puzzled and disgusted. Tina walked away for a peaceful afternoon with her half of the cigarettes. Hillary did not attempt to hide her disdain, and Maria giggled at the awkward air in the transit van.

"Really? Must you draw attention to us like that?"

"Shut up, woman, I didn't mean to. Come on now. We need a plan. We need a plan." He was bouncing on the seat and pulling his earlobe.

"Leave it to me," Hillary said, "I'll suss out the situation. We are not steaming in like vengeful gypsies. No, this needs a clever approach."

"We need to get him here. Tonight." Ronin said.

"Eh, him? Thought it was Anna you're after?" Maria asked.

"Indeed, we need to find her to lead us to someone more valuable."

"If I see that little bitch, I'll pick her up by the throat and chuck her in the back of this van." Ronin said.

"You certainly will not. The time for violence has passed. Now it's time for strategy. Let's just take a drive around the area, see what we can ascertain. A reconnaissance, if you will."

"What the hell are you talking about? Talk properly, woman."

"Just drive. Go past the woman's house. Do you understand?"

Ronin gritted his teeth and sneered, "You see what I've to put up with, Maria?"

"This is the street. Christine's house is the second last on that row, up there look." He pointed up the hill. "I'll tell you now, though, that woman won't tell me anything. I've been there before."

"No one's expecting her to. You're just the driver today, ok?" They passed slowly, looking for signs of occupants. "Go round again, drive around town a little, then back up."

Cars were parked tightly on the corner as the hill evened off. Maria held her breath as he squeezed the van through a tiny space. Then they came face to face with a car squeezing through in the opposite direction —the blue escort.

Hilary spoke from between still lips,

staring straight ahead. "Just wave and reverse. They don't know we're looking for him."

"I'm not reversing! It's my right of way!" he bounced on the seat, rapidly pointing at the others for them to reverse. His angry gestures were met simply by a stern shake of the driver's head.

"Just reverse and let them through, don't make a dam scene."

Ronin crunched the gears into reverse and leaned out of the window. He accelerated backward, up on the kerb, and scrapped along two parked cars. Metal grated and screeched as he dismounted with a thud and swung into a parking space. His face was bloated with blood as the rage pulsated. The blue escort drove slowly, the passengers observing the damage to the stationary cars, then giving the nod and a smirk to Ronin as they passed.

He punched the steering wheel, "I will get that bastard before they do. Just you watch."

"Come on," Maria squealed, "let's get away from here before anyone sees the mess of their cars."

Hillary watched the blue car in the side mirror. She watched them drive down the hill and past the house. She didn't detect any hesitation; they didn't slow down or stop too long at the bottom.

"Just turn up here and go back down, let's just watch for a while."

His crude 5 point turn bumped up on the kerb, and scraped the bumper of another car behind. Hillary rolled her eyes at Maria, who was biting her lips shut to keep the laughter in. They parked behind a Landrover and waited, not exactly out of sight, but discreet enough.

"Look, someone's coming out the door!" Maria's pointing hand was slapped down by Hillary's as quickly as it appeared.

"Sssh. Do you recognise him? Is he from around here?"

"Never seen him before, and that's definitely her house. That must be our man."

"Ok, everyone, stop looking, act normal."

Maria concentrated on biting her nails. Ronin dramatically checked the back of the van, while Hillary watched the man looking up and down the street, stepping out and throwing a black bag in the bin.

"Ok, let's go. We'll get a plan together and come back once it's dark."

"I'll just go and grab him by the neck right now!" Ronin rapidly pulled his earlobe.

"No!" Hillary said, "Leave this to me. We want to come out on top this time, yes?"

Claire

It was only a few meters to Jean's front door, but things were starting to feel very stressful. Claire pulled her hood over as she prepared to get out of the car. She didn't want any extra attention. She just had to stick to the plan and pray that Anna kept out of sight and away from trouble.

She felt a lot better knowing Bazz was ok in there. She'd always thought he was strange, but she was so very grateful for him. The new guilt twisting itself around her guts was that she didn't go in to see him. One day she would, but not yet. She smoked the last of her cigarette, composing herself, preparing for questions, and planning to act normal.

Wearing her hood like a horse wears blinkers, she fixed her eye on the door handle and headed straight for it. It felt like a dream, like running in sand, the handle not getting any closer. She reached out, then stumbled as the door opened before her. She fell in at Jean's feet, where she stood as if she'd been waiting there all day for her to return.

Claire felt the carpet under her palms. She lay on the pile of shoes and toys in the hall; all her energy was gone. Jean helped her up, and the safety of her house began to dispel her anxiety.

"Up you get, come on. Hang your jumper up, and come through. There's someone here to see you."

Claire warmed as she recalled her promise to play kerplunk with the boys tonight. She took her shoes off and put them together next to the door. She fixed her hair and looked at her exhausted face in the hall mirror, feeling her pulse subside. No more drama today - only some quality time with the boys, and then home to her own house tomorrow.

"Come on through then!" Jean shouted. Claire realised the house was strangely quiet. The boys would have run through to greet her by now, fighting for her attention. She tentatively pushed the door open, her calm destroyed again as the fear rose. There was someone next to Jean on the sofa.

Someone in a fluffy pink cardigan and tight acid-wash jeans.

The same cardigan she'd been wearing during every hospital visit.

But something was different now.

"Mum."

Irene smiled, more than she'd smiled in years. Her cheeks weren't exactly rosy, but they weren't electro therapy grey anymore either. Her hair was still wild, but in its natural color, all the black dye had grown out, leaving a mousy brown choppy bob.

"Surprise! When I knew you were coming, I called the hospital, and I arranged a home visit for your mum. I thought it would be good for us all to spend some time together." Jean said, with a look that begged a positive reaction from Claire. Her head tipped, and her eyebrows twitched as if willing her to applaud.

"It took a bit of convincing," Irene's voice wobbled, "but I've been doing so well, and when we explained that it was my only chance to see you, my key worker pulled some strings for me." Her eyes seemed to search Claire's face for recognition.

This was not part of Claire's plan for tonight. This was not part of her plan at all.

The same trickle of sweat took its path down her chest. The shaking started at her fingers, making its way up her forearms. Jean stood up and guided Claire to sit in her seat.

"The boys are staying at their Dad's tonight. I've fed them up with a fifty-pence mixture and some cheap cola, so they'll be making his life a misery for a change. I thought we could have a nice tea, maybe have a wee glass of wine together after."

Irene watched Claire's horrified expression at the mention of wine. "Not for me, Jeanie, I'm t-total. You two can enjoy yourselves, though. I'm just happy enough to see my sister and my daughter."

This was the most coherent Irene had been in a long time; Claire was equally as intrigued as she was repelled. She remembered bouts of enthusiasm and attention as she grew up, but they usually signaled a worse episode to come. She'd never been free to enjoy the brief happy times as they were filled with dread of what was brewing up. After a couple of nice days, it would follow that the curtains would be closed again, and the slightest creak of the floorboards would attract a furious tirade. "I don't fancy a drink either, but I'm happy for you to."

"Please yourselves. I've got a bottle of Lambrini, a big one too, and no bairns tonight, so I'll be treating myself."

Claire and Irene stared at each other, both incapable of making the first move. Jean raised her eyebrows at Claire, pushing her to make an effort, so she opened her mouth to say something, but it wouldn't come out. She felt like she'd never even known how to talk. Irene looked down at her socks and tried to pick a non-existent bit of fluff from her knee. Jean sucked air between her teeth and ran her hand through her cropped burgundy hair.

"So, Claire, why don't you tell your mum what you've been up to since the last time you saw her, and I'll get the tea on."

Irene's gaze was now direct and focused on Claire, she wasn't used to this. She couldn't remember the last time her mum had looked at her properly.

With Jean clattering around in the kitchen, only the estranged mother and daughter remained in the living room.

Eventually, Irene spoke. "I must have missed such a lot."

Claire nodded, "You've no idea."

Frankie

"The woman in the B and B said this was the place to go," Frankie said, squinting at the menu above the fryers in Cadoras chippy on the High Street.

"For a meal, I said, not a heart attack. What is this shit?" Billy peered into the glass hot-plate.

"2 fish lunches, darling."

"Suppers or single?"

"Lunch. 2 fish, please."

"Single or supper?"

Fish. And. Chips. For two people. Do you understand me?"

"Suppers then, aye?"

"Is lunch your supper in this godforsaken country?" Billy was starting to shout.

"Take a seat, and I'll bring them over." The waitress was unperturbed.

They slid into the booth; Billy wiped his finger along the surface and held it up to the light.

"This place is horrible. It's like we slid into a greasy time warp. It's nineteen fifty bloody eight in here. The state of this table." He picked at the edge of the grey marble coating.

"Go and order us a coffee while I phone the boss." Frankie dropped a handful of coins into Billy's hand and shooed him away. He slid his back to the wall and rested one leg on the bench. He lifted the Velcro flap and typed in the number he knew by heart.

One ring.

"Calling to give you an update, boss. Its..."

He nodded, and agreed, nodded again. He held the phone slightly away from his ear, occasionally wincing when the harsh language hit the spot or when the shrill consonants bit into his eardrum.

"I know... yes.... That's right... of course, boss."

"We have a car now, so just getting the lay of the land. Ok, ok.... Green street. Got it. As soon as I find them, I'll let you know."

He shook his head, "I promise I will call you as soon as I set eyes on them." He pressed the button, crunched the Velcro flap, and chucked the phone to Billy as he returned, pulling his stomach in to slide back into his seat.

"You can phone her next time."

"Deal, I'll do that, and you can order the food. At least the boss talks proper English. That girl up there doesn't even know what a latte is. All they've got is instant."

"After we eat this, we need to get out there and find Green Street."

"Did she tell you a number?"

"Nope, just the name."

The skinny-armed waitress wobbled under the weight of the two plates. A scattering of chips hit the floor in front of their table; she threw the plates down hastily to avoid dropping more.

"Thanks, darling," Frankie said, while Billy dismissed her with his hand, then lifted the yellow battered fish off its bed of chips by the tail. Vinegary steam rose, he was wary, but his stomach growled. He impaled four large chips at once and began shoving them in. He chewed loudly and breathed quickly, attempting to cool them down.

"The chips are decent." He blew tiny pieces of potato onto the table before prodding another three.

Frankie watched him digging in, his own fork still empty, "I will sleep on Green

Street if I have to. We need this job done; we stay up here too long we're gonna get heart disease."

Tina & Maria

"We need a new source of money. Things have really dried up since Hillary moved in. I want to go out to the club, and I want to get dressed up and dance. Not just sit about the shitty Viper Room hoping to get passed a warm tinny."

"What have we got that's worth any money?" Tina asked, then held her jewel-encrusted clown pendant up.

"No way, mum would kill us if we sold any of our jewelery," Maria replied.

"We could try babysitting again?"

"No chance, days of shitty nappies, crying toddlers and getting into bother for not looking after them properly, for fifteen quid. No thanks."

"You think of something then."

"I'm trying. It has to be something easy and quick."

"We could ask Dad for some money? It's not very easy, and would take a while sitting through the lectures about pulling our weight in the family again." Tina suggested as she applied mascara in the mirror.

"No, it's not worth the hassle." Maria sighed and rolled across the bed till she was flat on her back.

"Oh my god, I've got it! We could do a sponsored walk!" Tina's face lit up with her idea.

"That's not easy, or quick, and we need the money to buy drugs and vodka, not give it to fucking charity," Maria spoke in a slow, droning voice, not bothering to look or lift her head.

"We wouldn't actually do the walk, stupid, just get sponsored and keep the money! It's perfect! We'll look like nice thoughtful girls, and people will just give as loads of money for doing a good deed."

Maria rolled onto her front and rested on her elbows. "You're not as daft as you look Teeny-bop."

Standing in white blouses, with an empty jam-jar and an old jotter with the used pages ripped out, they looked quite the part. They'd split the pages into three columns; Name, Address, and Donation amount.

"Where will we say we're going to walk

then? Like how far? Will I write 10 miles?" Maria asked, chewing the pen.

"That's not enough, make it bigger, a mountain maybe. That would sound good."

"Shall I write Ben Nevis then?"

"Yeah, that sounds good, and it's in Scotland, so it's realistic."

"Let's start with Uncle James; he's got loads of money."

As they approach, they find him under a car, only visible from the thighs down. Tina shoves Maria to start talking.

"Uncle James, we need to ask you something." She bent a little to listen for his reply. He slid out on a low trolley, still lying down, he looked up at the smiling girls and said,

"No. Whatever it is," and slid back underneath. Tina pushed her again to keep trying.

"It's not for us. It's for charity. We're doing this thing, a sponsored walk. We need to collect some donations." Tina nodded and motioned her to keep going. "Just a small donation, every little helps, we're not asking for much."

He wheeled back out, getting up this time.

He looked at each girl in turn, dusted his hands off, and asked, "Where are you walking?"

"Ben Nevis," they said in unison, a sincerely as possible.

"And what's the charity?"

That hadn't crossed their minds. They looked at each other, then Tina said, "It's for an orphanage."

"It's such a shame, Uncle James, they don't have food or shoes or anything. Will you sponsor us to help the poor children?"

He smiled, dropping his arms and his guard, "well, let's see what I've got here." He patted his shirt pocket. "Oh yeah, I know what I've got, a good mind to drag you pair to your father and tell him you're conniving little brats. He grabbed each girl's shoulder, and twisted them around. He squeezed his fingers under their collar bones and dragged them a few steps along the grass. Maria squealed in pain, Tina shouted, "Wait, I know something worth more than that!"

He stopped but squeezed harder. Maria was crying now. "Let us go, and I'll tell you something really important, about Grandad."

James loosened his grip but didn't let go.

"What are you saying about my father? Don't you stoop to using his name for your nonsense!" He looked like he was about to cry.

"You remember the man that robbed him? Thingy McVay that ruined his life?"

He let them go, balled his fist, and gritted his teeth, "Andy McVay? How could I forget? That man destroyed my father."

"Ok, You forget about us, and anything we get up to, and I'll tell you where he is right now."

Maria stood weeping and holding her shoulder, but Tina stood straight. He took her in both hands, his fingertips burning into her shoulder blades.

"You tell me right now!" His eyes were becoming more bloodshot as he shook her.

"You promise to leave my sister and me to our own business." Her words strained through pain. He let her go, brushed his hands on his trousers as if brushing away the responsibility of hurting two girls half his age. "Tell me now, and you two can do as you please, but take your carry on away from the family."

Tina accepted, "Let's go for a little drive then. I'll point out the exact house where you'll find him."

CHAPTER FIVE

5

Claire

Jean poured her fourth glass of yellow wine. "I never thought I'd see the day my two best girls would be together in my house. I'm honestly over the moon." She picked another undercooked mini sausage roll from the bowl in the middle of the pine table. "What tape will I put on next? Do yous like Bruce Springsteen?"

Irene nodded, and Claire faked a smile. This was the kind of night she always wondered about. Now it was happening, she felt like an observer, like she wasn't inside her body. They'd covered the basic topics, jobs, the twins, dumped boyfriends, the annoying things about living with Anna.

Jean made them laugh with tales of the disgusting things the boys did and then gave Claire a red face by reminiscing about catching her with a boy behind the shed a few years ago.

"Honestly Irene, I thought it was a fox, or a badger, I went doon there with a rolling pin to cave it's heid in, and there she was with Scott. All I could see was his wee white bum cheeks going at it."

"Oh my god, Jean, shut up! You promised you would never bring that up again." Claire's face was scorching with embarrassment and a little anger.

Irene laughed, "It's ok, you don't need to hide anything from me."

"Aye, she's your mum, don't be shy," Jean added.

"Can you both stop talking about it now?" Claire's eyes were wide and her lips thin.

"Oh Claire, that expression! I remember it so well!" Irene said, "You made the very same face when I caught you with a crayon in your hand next to the scribbles on the new wallpaper." she looked warmed from the inside. Joy melted the lines between her eyebrows.

Claire laughed, "I remember that. You were laughing so much. But, then you smacked my bum, and then you started crying."

"I'm so sorry, Claire, I was a terrible mum to you. I really am sorry." The lines returned, cutting her forehead in two.

"Right guys, enough of that, let's get some good tunes on!" Jean interrupted, and Claire silently thanked her with a look.

As Jean drank her way down the giant bottle, she became engrossed in her own party. Swapping tapes, rewinding, and fast-forwarding to find 'the best bit.'

As the hours rolled on, the conversation flowed more easily between the sober pair.

"How did you end up so far away from her? Don't you miss the boys? I know how close you were with them."

"Sometimes, not even blood can keep people together. You of all people know that surely?" Claire felt instant guilt. She wanted to suck the words back and swap them for some soft, easy explanation. "I just mean, things happen, things change, life moves on." She looked up to the ceiling, praying for a reprieve.

Irene looked down at her glass and

swilled the dregs of fresh orange around the base. An awkward silence grew. Claire couldn't think of anything to fill it with, all the small talk was exhausted. She could sense Irene squirming in her seat. She could feel her eyes flitting between her face and the back of Jean's head. Irene leaned forward,

"I heard what happened in your house."

That trickle of sweat. Claire hid her trembling hands under the table.

"I wasn't there. It was some friend of Anna's, nothing to do with me. I just couldn't go back."

Irene's eyes, no longer weighed down by the bags of illness and hospital lighting, were watching closely and caught Claire's shaky reaction.

"So you didn't know him? The man that died on your living room floor?"

Claire's tortured heart cracked on the inside of her fragile rib cage. Her blood pressure forced her temples to thud so loud she thought everyone could hear. She'd played this question a thousand times a day since that night, planning her reaction, choosing the words that would portray her innocence. That question had finally been asked out loud, and now she was on the spot.

"No, not really, he was just some random that Anna's pal had a run-in with."

"It must have been horrible, happening in your house like that."

"Yeah, well, it's ok, it's fine. I mean I kind of wanted to move anyway." Claire stuttered, gulped, and wiped the sweat from her forehead.

"So it was for the best then? What happened?"

"What? No, how could someone getting their head smashed in with an iron be for the best?" Claire's voice cracked, and tears tingle behind her eyes.

"You got to start a new life, and you and I are here now, getting a fresh chance."

"That's sick. How could you say that?" Claire shakes her head, unable to believe she's hearing these words coming from her mum's mouth.

"You really don't know, do you?" Irene asked, slowly leaning in closer.

"What I do know is, I'm not listening to this. I'm going to bed." Claire pushed her chair out from the table. Irene put a hand on her hers to stop her.

"Listen to me. I've finally managed to drag myself out of that pit of depression, because the man that put me in there all those years ago is dead. He's got nothing over me now. He can't harm anyone from his place burning in hell." Irene's eyes were dark and intense; Claire broke away from her stare and shook herself free.

"I don't know what you're talking about. You sound crazy. Let me go."

"Shaun. The dead man in your house. It was him. He was your father."

Everything went quiet, Jean was still dancing, and the tape was still turning, but the edges of the room were blurring. She knew what was coming. Claire put her head between her knees and forced out deep rhythmical breaths. In… out… in… out… All she could hear was the blood whooshing through her ears as she thought back to the crack of the iron, the carpet beneath her knees, the smell of blood, his huge motionless body. His face. His hair. That cow's lick. Just like hers.

Frankie

"This car's got a funky smell, don't you

think?"

Frankie wrinkles his nose.

"Like what?"

"I dunno. Like animals or something."

"Have you looked in the back? It's covered in fucking dog hair."

"Why are we driving about reading every street sign? Why don't we just stop and ask someone?"

"Are you stupid?"

"Why not? It would save us time. And petrol."

"Ok, let's say we stop the next person we see. That old guy there."

"Go on, then he'll probably know the name of every street in this town."

"Let's say we stop him and ask, yeah? Then he tells us. That's great."

"Yeah, see, told you it's a good idea."

"Then he tells his mate about a couple of tasty-looking English geezers looking for Green Street."

"And?"

"Then his mate mentions this to another mate."

"Yeah, so?"

"Maybe his mate is McVay. Then we're fucked. He takes the girl and disappears again, and we are back to square one. We have to get it done here and get the rest. Do you fancy telling the boss that you messed it up?"

"Ok, let's just drive around. I ain't being that guy." Billy pulled the lace doily out of his black coat. He unwrapped the gun and placed it on his knee. Reaching into the other pocket, he pulled out four bullets. He rolled one between his thumb and forefinger while scanning for street signs.

"Put that away, for fuck sake. You really are on a mission, ain't you?"

"Yeah, what do you mean?"

"We are in a dodgy car we bought from a pikey, trying to find Andy fucking McVay to do some seriously dodgy business, and you bring that out in broad daylight. Put it away!"

"Stop stressing out. No one's looking at - Look! There! Look the bottom of that hill into that estate. Green Street. Take a left! You missed it! Go back!"

"I'll make the moves. I'm not braking and skidding into the street for everyone to see."

Anna

Anna arrives at Christine's with two cans of Tennant's and a tin of custard from Roy's spar. All the blinds and curtains were shut unusually tight. With no light escaping, the house looked abandoned. She hesitates at the gate, about to turn around. Maybe he's left already; it doesn't look like anyone's home. Maybe she shouldn't bother.

She pulls the hat she grabbed from Jean's hallway down over her ears and reminds herself why they bothered coming back up here in the first place. She wants to see him and get some answers. But she does still hate him a bit, and probably like to hit him over the head with her bag of tins.

She gets to the front door but can't bring herself to knock. She raises her hand, drops it, and raises it again. She was already 15 minutes late, so she stood a while longer, just to give him a little taste of his own medicine. Quarter of an hour's not much of a trade-off for missing half her life, but she wanted to give him even the slightest taste of abandonment.

A few minutes passed, and she heard a few coughs from inside, so he was definitely there. She was shivering now, her breath like steam engine trail from between her chattering teeth.

She knocked on the door with her numb knuckles and held her breath till it opened.

"Anna! Come in, is that the time already? In you come."

He opened his arms, smiling wide. She looks at the ground and shuffles past him in the dark hallway. The living room is also in darkness, so she follows the light into the kitchen.

"Where's Christine? Why's it so dark in here?" Anna asks, looking at the oven tray with 24 fish fingers on it.

"She went out to give us some time to get to know each other again. Now, tea? Coffee? Something stronger?"

"I'll make my own tea. You don't know how I like it." She said, turning away from him.

"What's in the bag?" He asked, clearly struggling for ideas.

"Oh, here, you still drink beer, right?" She held the bag at arm's length, not making eye contact.

"Thanks, I don't drink these days, but I do love custard."

As the kettle boils, Anna looks around Christine's kitchen. Its familiarity is comforting and distracting - the egg cups on the shelf, the plates on the wall with peppers painted on them, and the printed canvas with different kinds of bread. She takes it all in slowly, feeling more and more uncomfortable as he stares at her from the side.

"You look just like your mum, you know?" He said, almost whispering.

"So I hear."

"Look, I'm glad you came back tonight. It means a lot to me. I've wasted so much time, and I want to make it up to you."

"Well, let's see, that will be nine birthdays, nine Christmases, six parents evenings..." her voice trembled as tears rolled from her eyes, her bottom lip turned out, and her body began to shake. He wrapped his arms around her, silent, until the sobs stopped.

"Why did you come back now? Why not five years ago? What's changed?"

"Well, I've wanted to come back. I think about you all the time. I always wonder what you're up to, if you're happy. But, like I said earlier, things are complicated. I don't know how much your mum mentioned about my situation..."

"Situation? She didn't mention anything. She was too busy being terminally ill, not that you cared." More tears stung her cheeks.

"I'm sorry. I'm sorry about Debbie, I'm sorry I wasn't there for you, but I'm here now. I just got myself in a lot of trouble up here, I got involved with some people I shouldn't have, did some things I shouldn't of, and it made it impossible to come back."

Anna wanted to say, me too! And tell him all about Archie, Shaun, Davie, the pikeys, and the money. She just nodded, conceding nothing could be changed. She accepted his small apology.

"I'm going to wash my face. You can put those in the oven now," she pointed at the excessive portions on top of the cooker.

"Wait! Hold on," he started to cough, one hand over his mouth, one hand blocking her way. "Stay there a minute." He closed the kitchen door behind him and coughed all the way up the stairs. Anna stood baffled; maybe he'd left dirty clothes in the bathroom or something worse. She cringed and waited till he returned, breathless from running up and down the stairs.

In the bathroom, she ran a sink full of hot

water and tested the scent of various soaps. She wanted to waste some time and think of things to talk about. Dewberry, Voseine, or Matey? She laughed at the pirate-shaped bottle and Christine's odd choices, then poured some in the sink and gave it a swirl. The smell reminded her of Sunday nights, flannel nighties, and watching All Creatures Great and Small, way back when he was still around. She wondered if he'd remember, but she wouldn't ask in case he couldn't. That would be worse than wondering.

She dried her face, pushed the damp strands away from temples, and looked in the mirror at her jumper. The neck was soaked with tears and soapy water. Her cuffs were soggy, and a drip ran down inside to her elbow, quickly turning cold. She'd borrow a fleece from Christine's room and leave hers to dry on the heater.

She opened the door and flicked the light on. Someone was in there, she screamed, they screamed. Anna pulled the door shut and held the handle. Inside the room, the screams continued; Andy ran up the stairs and opened the door with Anna's hand still attached to it. He held the screaming intruder till she calmed down. Anna looked at the person who'd been sitting in the dark in Christine's room, with her long lost Dad stroking her head.

"Anna, this is Alice, your little sister."

CHAPTER SIX

6

Hillary

"Don't say anything to make them suspicious." Ronin said, "We just need to get them out of the house."

"Yes. I know this. It was my idea remember." Hillary checked her lipstick in the mirror, then gave her fringe a quick blast from her mini tin of Elnett hair spray.

He coughed and covered his eyes, "Why do you have to spray that shit in here? It's choking me woman!"

"Oh, do stop whining."

"Do you think they'll definitely fall for it?"

"Of course, no one can resist a missing

dog! Or a crying woman needing help. They'll both be out on the street shouting for little Scruffy, and you can get whichever one of them comes nearest and throw them into the back of the van."

"I don't care which one it is, father or daughter, both of them will get me a payout somehow."

"You've got the rope and the sack, right?" she asked, lighting a cigarette.

"Why are you smoking in here? It bloody stinks. Did those two wee brats get you smoking?"

"My having a little puff on a cigarette in a time of stress isn't worth moaning about, is it? Come on. We have more important things to concern us. Like you being capable of catching someone and tying them up without causing a big scene. Do you think you can do this?"

"Aye, of course I can. Just you get out there and do your bit. Nice defenseless lady, that needs help; you're good at playing that part, eh?"

She blew smoke in his face and watched him gasp, then got out of the van, "Be ready to catch one of them, and don't mess this up." She slammed the door and approached the house with an extra swing in her hips as he watched her.

Anna

"How old is she?" Anna asks her father.

"I'm eight." Alice's little face turns up to Anna, smiling.

"So, this is how things got complicated, is it? Did my mum know?"

"That's all in the past," Andy held both hands out, "now's the time for fresh starts. Didn't you always wish for a little sister?"

Anna shrugged, secretly pleased that he'd remembered this little bit from her childhood, but furious and shocked still.

"I always wanted a big sister, didn't I, dad?" Alice said, resting her head on his arm.

"That's right darling, and here she is."

"So is this the real reason you came? Because of her? Not for my benefit, but for hers, because she wanted a big sister?"

Alice starts to cry and buries her head in Andy's side.

"For both of you. For all of us, we are family."

"Family? I don't need a family. I've been

fine this far without one."

Alice is howling now, "I thought you said she was nice and would be the best sister ever?"

"How would he know that?" Anna laughed, hiding the pain, "He's not seen me for half my life. He has no idea what kind of person I am."

Andy strokes Alice's hair, "I know she's nice because you remind me of her, every day." He spoke softly, into the top of her head, but he looked at Anna.

"She's kind to animals like you. She likes to stick up for people that are getting bullied, just like you."

Anna folds her arms and looks at the ground, swallowing hard.

"She likes having fun like you. She likes drawing, and so do you. She likes playing games and always wished for someone to play them with; I remember that."

"Do you like games? What about snap? I brought cards with me." Alice wipes her nose on Andy's sleeve.

"Why don't you two sit at the table here, and have a little game while I cook our meal?"

"Can we?" Big brown eyes and a freckled

button nose look up at Anna. She wanted to tell her no; she doesn't have time for silly games. She came here to find out why her dad was such an arsehole, and tell him what she thought of him. But looking down, she could see herself at 8. No one could have said a bad word about her dad back then. She didn't know at that age that dads could just disappear, and maybe Alice didn't need to hear that right now. Perhaps a few minutes wouldn't hurt.

"Ok, just one game then."

Anna watches her little hands shuffle the cards. Some fall out, and others turned the wrong way. The pile is spreading wider and messier.

"Here, I'll show you a better way." She takes the cards, swiftly rearranges them into a neat deck, then deals two piles. Her belly rumbles as the food smell swirl into her nostrils.

"Where does Christine keep the sauce then?" Andy asks as he prepares the table. He stops, puts a finger to his lips. "Shhh," he whispers, "I think I heard the gate." He and Alice stay still, wide-eyed, breath held.

"It's probably just Christine," Anna states,

flipping a card over.

Knock Knock.

Andy points to the cupboard under the stairs; he mouths, "Go, go now!"

Alice slips from her seat and into the darkness.

"Eh, what are you doing?"

Andy grabs Anna's arm, pulling her towards the cupboard." Please, stay with her in there, till I say. Just do it please, I'll explain after." She would never usually accept such a bizarre instruction without question, but the look on his face forced her to give him the benefit and oblige.

Alice squeezes her hand and pulls her in. The door closes, blinding them in pitch black. Anna sits on what feels like a toolbox, straining to hear what's going on in the hall. Her heart pounds; she feels around in the dark for Alice. She's completely silent, wedged into the far corner behind the brush and mop. She rests a hand on her tiny shoulder, feeling her warmth.

"What are we doing in here?" Anna whispered.

"We always do this when someone comes to the door, don't you?"

"Em, yeah, sometimes. Not for a while."

As much as she wasn't interested in the girl, she didn't want to shatter her illusions of normality.

He hadn't answered the first; another knock came.

It felt as if the building was holding its breath. She wanted to burst through the door and ask what the fuck was going on.

She listened to nothing, waiting, breathing in smells of polish and windowlene. Finally, there was a tiny floorboard creak, then a squeak of the door opening.

"It's ok. It was just some woman. I watched her leave through the peephole; out you come."

Anna squints under the kitchen lights, readjusting from the dark. She looks at her dad properly for the first time. He meets her eyes and shakes his head almost imperceptibly and mouths "please." She knows what this means. It can wait till later. She'll get answers once Alice is out of the way.

"Right, you girls, get that game started, and I'll check on the chips."

Anna's impressed at his ability to pretend nothings wrong, so she goes along with it, guessing that's where she inherited those skills from.

"Ok, I'll deal the cards, and you start this time." She shuffles again, looking over the top of Alice's head, watching his movements. He's got the blinds rolled all the way down, and tucked into the side of the window sill, leaving no cracks. He taps the fish slice on the countertop. Fast and nervous.

Knock Knock.

"Fuck sake," Andy said, "she's back again. She must have seen the kitchen light or something. In the cupboard quick."

Alice takes Anna's hand and tries to pull her towards the hiding place.

"I'll just answer it," Anna said, pushing past, "I'll tell her Christine's not in." Andy waved his hands and shook his head violently,

"Nooooo!"

"Don't be bloody stupid. Whoever it is will just keep knocking if they think someone's in." Anna reached for the door while Andy ducked into the darkness behind. She shook her head and tutted at his over-the-top reaction. She'd just tell this woman to come back later, and once she was gone, she'd get to the bottom of her father's ridiculous behavior. She released the chain and turned the yale; from the other side, a hand thumped on the wood. She pushed and held it back.

"McVay!" A rough, angry voice shouted from outside, the weight against the door doubled. Her stomach twisted as she frantically pushed against the wood, trying to get the chain back on. Why the hell didn't she check first? She looked over her shoulder, hoping for her dad to appear and help her push the door back against whoever was trying to get in, but he'd disappeared, left her to deal with it alone. The weight became too much, her feet were sliding backward on the carpet, her arms shaking until they collapsed and the door swung open.

One after another, after another, big, huge, angry men pushed into the hall. Anna fell onto the stairs as they poured into the hall. The lights were switched on, and they swung hammers, golf clubs and fists. Square edges of heads and angry black eyes filled the house. Anna couldn't feel her legs, bile rose up into her throat. They'd found her. They'd come for Ronin's money. This was it.

"Where's McVay?" A dark-haired,

monster of a man grabbed her throat and pushed her onto the staircase. His teeth were exposed, his lips curled back, she could see a yellow furry coating, his gums were red. She shook her head. He pulled her to her feet by the collar. He slammed her into the wall and pushed her chin up with a hammer. Other men kicked open the doors upstairs; more were shouting in the living room. Anna shook her head and looked hard into his dark eyes, "I don't know what you're talking about." He pushed her jaw harder with the cold metal, she kept her eyes on his.

Beep beep beep beep beep beep… the smoke alarm stuns them all still. His grip loosens, he looks around, confused. They've all stopped shouting. No one knows what's going on…

Beep beep beep beep...

Anna's ears are throbbing. Someone shouts from the kitchen,

"The back door's open, come on, out this way!"

The man holding her against the wall is disorientated, the noise is making him cower. Anna tries to push him away, but he's huge and much stronger. He throws her back against the wall and raises the hammer, about to strike; Anna closes her eyes. This is it. In that fraction of a second, she thinks of her mum, and of Claire, and all the things they haven't done yet; they should never have come back here. She holds her breath, ready for impact. He pushes her chest, then lets go.

She opens her eyes and crumbles to the floor, watching his back as he follows the rest of the men shoving and shouting out of the back door through the smoke-filled kitchen.

She closes her eyes, stays on her knees. With her ears pulsating and the alarm blaring, she rubs the back of her head.

She opens her eyes again to an empty house. All the doors are open, cold wind blows through, and the fire alarm screams above her head. She runs to the kitchen, pulls her sleeve over her hand, and grabs the grill handle. The blackened fish fingers smoke as she throws the whole thing out into the back garden. She flaps a tea towel under the alarm till it goes off. The relief mixed with adrenaline makes her head spin.

She opens the cupboard under the stairs, "Dad, are you in there?"

Alice crawls out from the back of the darkest corner, tears rolling down her round face.

"Dad, just come out; they're gone."

"He's not in here," Alice howls.

"Well, he can't of gone fa. He'll be back," Alice said in a soft, careful tone, kneeling beside Alice and drying her eyes with her sleeve. Before she can answer, car tires screech to a halt outside, a police siren wails and blue flashes light up the hallway where they crouch, hearts thumping.

"Get back in the cupboard for a minute. Let me check, ok? I'll be straight back."

Jackson

“How many times are we going to drive round in the same circle? I feel like I’m getting seasick,” Jamie asked, his voice rolling around like a drunk’s.

“They’re staying in the Ashvale; we know that. They’ll leave there some time, and when they do, we’ll know about it.”

“Can’t we just sit outside the B and B? Honestly, I feel like I’m going to throw up.”

"Nope, I'm going between the bank, the post office, and here. You know why?"

"Because you hate me and want me to be ill?" Jamie moaned.

"This isn't about you Jamie. I have a feeling. A hunch, and a strong one at that, that they are up here to rob somewhere. They probably think banks up north have less security. Soft targets for a heist. I'm going to watch them casing out the bank, or maybe the post office, and I'm going to catch them."

"Did someone tell you this, or…"

"I don't need anyone to tell me. My intuition is never wrong."

"Oh my goodness!" Jamie covered his eyes with his hands.

"What? What is it?"

"Look down there! Down the hill, there's people on the road! It looks like a fight, oh no!" Jamie yelped as Jackson hit the siren and raced towards the crowd.

"Open the window! Put the flashing light on the roof, quickly!"

Jamie struggled with the tangled wire; it slipped from his hand as she turned a sharp right to block the road. The magnet stuck to his door; he leaned out, trying to free it while still held in position by his seat belt.

As she braked, the tires screeched, and the crowd dispersed, leaving a body on the road.

Jackson jumped out and ran to the scene. She felt for a pulse and radioed for an ambulance and back up. Behind her, Jamie pulled the light from the door and placed it on the roof.

From the next street, Jackson heard a heavy diesel vehicle accelerate quickly. She scanned the area - no weapons visible, no other onlookers apparent.

Caucasian male, early to mid-fifties, not someone she recognised.

"Jamie, come down beside him, try and establish some communication till the ambulance arrives."

"Ew, there's blood on his face."

"Get on with it. I'm going to look around, see if anyone's been watching."

"Oh my god, what if they come back?"

"Jamie, we are the fucking police! We'll arrest them! Just wait there, ok?" Jackson turned in a full circle, looking beyond the immediate area, looking for people or lights.

At the end of the terrace, second house down, a door ajar, someone looking out from the darkness. She walked straight towards them.

Frankie

"I dunno why you thought you'd find a kebab shop open at this time. We should have just eaten that shit the old dear offered us."

"I'm not eating anything else she cooks. That chunk of gristle bouncing between my teeth was enough to give me nightmares. What kind of person puts a whole chicken carcass in a pan of soup. All those grotty little brown bits floating about, the grease pools on top. Na, fucking give me a tin of Heinz any day."

"Well, it's too late. There's nothing open. Just eat that sandwich you got from the garage."

Billy sighed and ripped the top off the triangular box, tossing it into the back seat.

"I'm gonna take a drive round past our target. We need to act soon, so let's get a feel for the place in the dark."

"Why do they insist on putting tomato straight onto the fucking bread? This is disgusting. A ploughman's lunch? Fucking idiots, they could have put the tomato in between the lettuce and the cheese, like a little barrier, to keep the bread dry, but oh no, that would be too fucking easy, wouldn't..."

"Shut up about your belly for once, look down there. That's Andy on the road." Frankie turned the lights off and drove in darkness towards the flashing blue outside Christine's house, pulling in behind a car at the top of the road.

"How do you know it's him?" Billy asked, throwing a slice of tomato out the window.

"Do you know anyone else that wears beige chinos?" he points to the body on the road. They observe the scene, the concerned woman at his head, the two police officers staying close, then the ambulance wheeling him in.

"Where's the kid then? Ah, don't say we lost her!"

"Na, she'll be safe somewhere. She always is. Don't worry about her for now, it's him we need to get a hold of, and it's pretty obvious where he's going to be."

"Where?" Billy asked, picking a bit of lettuce from between his teeth.

"The fucking hospital, you idiot!"

Anna

Anna stepped out to meet the approaching police officer. She recognised her instantly, those big watery eyes and round face.

"What happened? Is that my dad down there?"

"Anna, I was hoping you could tell me. What's been going on here tonight?"

"I don't know. I don't know anything. Just let me see my dad." She pushed past and ran down onto the road. She got on her knees by his shoulder, frost twinkled, and steam rose from the puddle of blood under his head.

"Dad, Dad, please, wake up."

"Anna..." his eye's opened a little, "don't let anyone see her..."

"I'll come with you to hospital."

"No, stay, look after her." He squirmed in pain, she squeezed his hand.

He drifted in and out, closing his eyes for longer each time,

"Dad, don't leave me now. You've only just come back." She took off the fleece, rolled it in a ball, and put it under his head.

She couldn't feel the cold now, but her lips were blue, and her teeth rattled.

The ambulance arrived to a street lined with onlookers. Porches, steps and pavements were full, like a street party in the middle of winter. DI Jackson and her partner held the crowd back as the paramedics got to work with their equipment. They wrapped him in a foil blanket, sealed an oxygen mask over his face and wheeled him into the sterile white light in the back of the ambulance.

"I'm going to need to talk to you properly about what went on tonight, Anna."

"I told you, I don't know, I've no idea, I didn't see anything. I just came out when I heard your siren."

"How long's your dad been back? Interesting that he should show up, and there's trouble, don't you think?"

"Look, I've told you, I can't tell you anything because I don't know."

"So you didn't see the altercation? And you've no idea who the other parties involved were?"

"No, no idea."

"I'm going to let you have a think about it over night. If any details come back to you once the shock has subsided, we'll discuss it tomorrow. Ok? You give my colleague your contact details, and I'll be in touch."

Anna nodded and waited for Jamie to get his notebook ready.

The street returned to burnt orange darkness as the ambulance drove away. Anna avoided eye contact with any of the spectators and double-stepped back into Christine's. She locked both the doors and checked each room while figuring out what to say to the strange child she was now in charge of.

"You can come out now. It's ok," she held the door wide open to let a little light in. No reply came.

"Alice, are you in there? It's ok to come out now." Calling into the silence, an unusual feeling of fear caught Anna from nowhere; she got onto her knees and crawled into the darkest corner, feeling for a small warm arm or leg. She could feel smooth plastic, a mop bucket, the ironing board, a cold, hard hoover. Then she heard a tiny whimper from behind it all. She reached a hand in behind the barricade and felt Alice's shaking hands wrapped around her knees.

"Is dad dead now?" the tiny, sad voice asked from the darkness.

"No, he'll be fine, don't worry. He's safe. The doctors are looking after him." Anna dismantled the fence of cleaning tools and took her hand.

"Do you like ice-cream? The fish fingers are ruined, but Christine usually has some raspberry ripple in the back of her freezer."

"I do like ice-cream, actually." Alice replied.

Looking down at her tear-stained face, Anna saw her dad's eyes, younger and untainted, but the same. "Why don't you get some pajamas on, and I'll sort out the snacks ok?" Alice ran up the stairs while Anna tried to get the house back to an acceptable state before Christine got home. She straightened the stools, hung up the picture back up in the hall, and hooked the curtain back onto its pole.

Anna's stomach was tight with guilt. She could barely look at Alice, tucked into the corner of the sofa, eating ice-cream, when it was her fault their dad was in hospital alone. It felt like she was wearing a belt three holes too tight. She sat on the footstool, holding space between two slats of the blinds. She prayed for Christine to come home; she needed her to take charge and look after this child.

She needed to get out of there, to go to his bedside and tell him she was sorry. Tell him that it was all her fault. It was her that crossed the Dougherty's, and it should never have been him that got hurt. She should never have come. None of this would have happened. The belt of guilt tightened its grip around her as she saw Alice's eye get heavy. She was forcing herself to stay awake, waiting for her dad to come back. That wasn't going to happen tonight.

"Why don't you have a wee lie down? I'll wake you up when he gets in. You can brush your teeth in the morning, ok?"

Alice nodded a slid easily into sleep. Anna tiptoed over, straightened her blanket, and pulled away the sticky strands of hair from her chin. She sat at the other end of the sofa, watching her sleep, prepared to get her into the cupboard if Ronin's family came back to finish the job they started.

CHAPTER SEVEN

7

"What the fuck has been going on in here?" Christine was six inches from Anna's face; she must have dozed off.

"It looks like a fucking army's marched through this house! And why's my back garden covered in fish fingers?"

Anna points at Alice, reminding Christine there was a sleeping child next to them, then points to the kitchen.

She rubs her eyes and stumbles through, "I'm so glad you're back. I don't know where to start. It just happened..."

"Spit it oot hen, what happened? Where's Andy? He's no left you babysitting, has he? I'll kill him..."

"No, it's not his fault. He's in hospital. It

was the Dougherty's, there was loads of them, they just burst in,"

"Oh god no. Is he ok? I should of known this would happen."

Anna rests her elbows on the countertop, sinking her head into her hands, "It's all my fault. I should never have come," tears drop off the end of her nose.

"Your fault? It's his fault. He should of known they wouldn't forget what he did."

"What he did? It was me! I stole Ronin's money. It's me they're after." She looked at Christine from between her fingers covering her face.

"No, no. They bastards obviously heard he was in town and came to give him what for. It's been years, but they won't have forgotten." Christine sprayed bleach over every surface, elbowing Anna out of the way. She leaned on the fridge instead.

"So they were after him? Not me?"

"You never heard about his history with them?"

"No. What did he do?" Anna dragged the hair off her face, trying to take in this new information.

"Let them down, stole from them, double-crossed them, lied, disappeared, who knows? Take your pick. You don't know the half of what he's capable of, hen."

"So is this why he never came back? Did my Mum know about it?"

"It's probably one of many reasons," Christine scrubbed the worktop without looking up, "You're mum knew alright, she had a tough time convincing them she didn't know where he was. Poor Debbie, they were never away from your door after he left."

"I don't even remember that." Anna was confused, like a big piece of a puzzle was missing.

"Your Mum wanted to protect you from Andy's crap. You were just a kid. Honestly, Anna, you don't know what that man's capable of."

"Well, he's capable of having a secret child and forgetting about his first one, so..." Anna tried to laugh, but it gurgled into a sob.

"Oh Christ, I didnae even ask! How did it go when he introduced you? Was it a shock?" Christine stopped scrubbing, and her scowl melted. "She's a lovely wee thing, isn't she?"

"For a start, he didn't introduce me, I accidentally found her hiding in your room, and I'm not really bothered about her."

"Really? You're not bothered? That's a shame. She's been awfy excited to meet her big sister."

"I don't even know her, and I wouldn't class her a sister."

"Give it time, I know it's a shock, but she needs you."

"She's got him. She doesn't need me. And I don't need them."

Christine stood silent, in her way that pulled words from Anna that she didn't want to say.

"What? I don't. I'm fine without them. I just came to get answers from him; that's all I need. I need to go to the hospital and see him. He made me stay and look after her, but I can't. I can't look after her, can you? Can you watch her while I go?"

"Ok, you need to calm down Anna, take a deep breath."

"I need to go now, please?"

Christine passed the warn dry jumper from the heater and gave her a tenner from her purse.

Anna

It was long past visiting hours, and most of the hospital was in darkness. She had a rough idea where he'd be. She'd been here before, late at night with an empty feeling and no idea of what her future held anymore. Here she was again, uncertain and tired.

She smoked a cigarette at the door, shivering and listing what she had to say. She didn't know what was important or what was petty. Things she'd wanted to know for years seemed irrelevant now he was actually there.

The tall ashtray was overflowing, beneath the cigarette ends was solid with icy water. She rolled her train ticket inside her pocket, picking the torn edge. The automatic doors slid open with every hesitant step forward, and closed again as she declined their warm invitation, having second, third, and fourth thoughts.

The heat from the A and E waiting room eventually became irresistible, and she entered, gasped, then slid straight into a corner behind a vending machine and pulled a large fake olive tree in front of her.

Taking up all the seats at the front of the room, watching the admissions desk, and looking straight at the entrance to the ward. Five huge square heads all in a row, different heights, and hair colours, but unmistakably Dougherty. Were they waiting for her Dad? Or her? Or one of their own? Either way, this was bad. Really bad.

She should have eaten more than just ice-cream today. Her hands were tingling, painful as they heated up, her heart was punching her insides, and her legs were wobbling. She slid down the wall, onto her haunches, and wrapped her arms around her knees.

She had to know if he was dead or alive. She had to ask why he'd never come back, and she needed to know what the fuck was going on.

If she could get into the corridor without being seen, she could definitely find him. She'd seen plenty of American versions of this scenario on TV; she needed to find a nurse, steal her uniform and walk confidently from bed to bed till she found him.

Then she remembered this was real life, and she'd just have to make a run for it. She popped her head round the side of the vending machine. Including the five deadly gypsies, there were nine people altogether. Someone would stop her, so bursting through the triage door in jeans and a jumper wasn't going to work either. Stepping back into her hiding place, she reminded herself she'd been in horrible situations before and always thought of something.

But she couldn't think now. She had too much adrenaline, and she was too hungry. Her head was spinning as she grasped for ideas. She couldn't wait in this corner all night. Her heart was aching, and the acid in her empty stomach bubbled. She remembered the promised fish fingers and salad cream. The burnt fish fingers.

That was it.

She looked up at the roof, polystyrene squares held in a thin metal frame, a CCTV camera facing the entrance, a sprinkler system of little rosettes and copper pipes, and two smoke detectors in diagonal corners. Near the desk, on the wall, was a red squared 'break glass in emergency,' but it was way beyond the danger area. She had to make this happen another way.

The plastic tub holding the artificial tree had brown stones in place of soil. They were dusty, with a scattering of orange crumbs and a soft watsit on top. With a handful ready, she got into a sprinting position, just edging the corner of her hiding place, and took aim with her hand. Three of the pebbles were lined up on the buffed lino floor. With her thumb and finger poised, aiming for the wall beneath the desk, she took a deep breath and pinged.

The first one had no effect. It slid a few feet and sat there.

For the second attempt, she readied her hand, building tension till it was painful, then released. It skimmed the floor like a stone on the ocean, bouncing on its path to the front. It hit, with a quiet pop. Just enough to draw the attention of a woman with her burnt hand in a plastic bag. She peered at it, looking for a moment like she might stand up. Anna prepared to run. The woman simply closed her eyes and held the bagged hand to her chest.

With the next pebble lined up, she used two fingers to flick for extra momentum. This time it bounced once, and hit the wall with a ding loud enough to turn three heads. The middle man of the five got off his seat and moved towards the spinning pebble.

Anna took the chance while all eyes were on him. She slid out from behind the tree and glided to the opposite corner, where she crouched behind a leaflet stand. She could hear a few mumbles, but daren't look. She waited for the quiet to return, then took the remains of her train ticket from her pocket. She lit the corner, but it went straight out. She lit it again, and blew this time. Charred edges fluttered to the ground as it glowed red in her hand. She blew again, encouraging the smoke to swirl, then she bit her lip and tiptoed underneath the smoke detector. She wobbled on her stretched feet, waving the smouldering ticket under the tiny flashing light.

Beeeep beep beeeeep beep beeeep

Crouching back down behind the leaflet stand, she listened to the chaos ensue; chairs scraping on the floor, panicked voices, a tannoy announcement - barely audible over the wailing alarm. Feet rushed past her hiding place and beyond. Through the glass exit doors, she could see the floodlit concrete filling up with people, nurses, wheelchairs, and people dragging infusion bags on metal stands.

The waiting room was empty now, her

path clear. She ran straight for the triage door and into the maze of corridors beyond. She had to stay unseen till they brought everyone back in, and she knew where to go.

The chapel door was always open, and no one was ever in there.

She slid into the dimly lit room and positioned herself behind one of floor-length burgundy curtains. Despite the ear-piercing alarm, the room still felt strangely tranquil.

She stood tight to the wall, breathing shallow. With the curtain touching her face, she remembered childhood games of hide and seek, praying to become invisible while desperate to giggle.

She'd once spent a lot of time in this room, with its wooden benches and burgundy velvet. She'd eaten sad-looking sandwiches in there, she'd done an entire Barbie colouring book in there, she'd stolen candles from there and occasionally even slept in there. All while waiting for her mum to die.

The smell made her feel 15 again, but she didn't have time to open any of those boxes right now. She had the present to worry about.

The alarm stopped, leaving her in a

silence so heavy she felt she could touch it. She listened as beds and trolleys rolled and rattled past. Conversations came and faded out along the corridor till finally calm was restored.

She knew where the ICU beds were, and she could easily find the emergency admissions ward. He'd be in one of those, she was sure.

Jackson

DI Jackson waves off the last fire engine and scratches her head under her hat.

"What a night. Nothing happens for months, then Anna and her father turn up, and all hell breaks loose."

"So what did the firemen say?" Jamie's mouth opens into a huge black yawn.

"No fire, just smoke."

"So it could have just been a cigarette?"

"It could. But I doubt it. There's something more to it than that. I'm going in to look at the CCTV video."

"What now? But it's past midnight! I was supposed to finish my shift at ten. I've already gone above and beyond tonight."

"Crime doesn't have a clocking off time Jamie. I want to see who's been in and out of here tonight. As long as Andy McVay is in that building, it's of interest to us."

"Seriously? You're going to keep us up all night, looking for a sneaky cigarette smoker? You're going to waste your time looking for some old guy who's been rolling up in the toilets when we've got those Swindon guys to keep an eye on?"

"Dam, I forgot about them!"

"Well, I suggest we go home, get a good night's sleep and prioritise our workload tomorrow."

"Our workload?"

"Yes, don't you want me to come? I thought this was our secret project? I mean, if you want someone else, you just have to say, but they might make you tell the Sargent about that Swindon call. It's up to you..."

"Yes, that's what I meant, good, our workload. Me and you. Tomorrow."

"Ooh fun. I'll bring snacks."

Anna

Anna follows the sound of his rattling cough past all the blue curtains. She passes beeps, groans and the swoosh of a ventilator. The three night staff are crowded round a magazine and eating biscuits at the end of the ward.

She pulls the next curtain back a fraction and slips in. She watches him lying there, head bandaged up like a cartoon character. There's a drip in his hand and an oxygen mask, hanging ready, under his chin. His eyes are still closed, his chest heaves, preparing to cough again. His shaking hand reaches for the mask. She doesn't know what to do. Her feet are welded to the ground. The half of her that wants to hug her dad, is suffocated by the half that's too furious and terrified.

"Anna, my girl, are you ok? Where's Alice?" He tries to sit up, but doesn't have the strength.

"Shhh, she's fine; Christine's looking after her." She whispered and hesitantly put her hand on his forearm. "What happened tonight?"

"It was years ago, ten years. Something happened with old James Dougherty. We were partners for a bit, but it went wrong, but don't worry."

"Don't worry? You know they were out there, waiting for you? They're not finished with you yet. What are we going to do?"

"Give me your hand," he said, offering his weak arm, "I need you to help me with something. It's important we do it fast."

"What is it? I'm already in trouble with the Dougherty's. I thought they'd come for me."

"You? Why would they want to hurt you?"

"I kind of owe money to one of them, it's a long story, but if they catch up with me, I'm in big trouble."

"Oh my girl," he squeezed her hand, "we need to get this done. We need to leave this place and that family behind."

"What is it?"

"It needs to happen tonight. I was going to do it, but I'm stuck in here. I'm in no fit state to dig anything just now. I need your help."

Anna sighed and patted his arm gently, "You've had a bump on the head Dad, you're not thinking straight. Why don't you get some sleep, and I'll come back tomorrow."

"Our old house, next door to Christine's, it's in the garden." The heart monitor at his bedside fluctuated faster.

"You're delirious, dad. I'm going to go. I'll come back..."

"No," he pulled her arm, looked hard into her eyes as the monitor flashed quickly, "I buried money in our old garden, and I need you to help me dig it up before the Dougherty's come back. Before, before... anything else happens."

"Money. I see. That's why you came back. You weren't looking for me at all. It makes sense now. How fucking stupid was I to think you'd come back to find me!" She drew her hand from his.

"I came back to give the money to you. It's the least I can do. I put it there for the future. For your future. The time's come to share it. Will you help me?"

"You don't think I could of done with a wee sub when I was fucking orphaned at 15? You don't think I've been on my arse the last ten years? Me and mum scrimped and saved and went without, now you're telling me there's money in the garden?" Her angry whispering was getting too loud. She stopped, leaned in, and quietly said, "I wish you'd never even come back." She shook her head and turned to leave.

"There's over a hundred grand there, and half of it's for you." He sputtered, before she opened the curtain.

Of course, she couldn't believe him. He was full of shit, always was. She remembered listening to her mum saying he lived in a fantasy land. She remembered Christine telling her to take anything he said with a pinch of salt.

But fifty grand? That was worth getting her hands dirty to check. She froze, staring at the curtain, still listening for approaching nurses.

"Ok," she said, "I'm in."

It's 2 am when Anna asks Christine for a spade.

"That fucking bastard! After all these years? And you believe him?"

"I don't know, but I'm going to find out." Anna's pupils are huge, her voice wobbles.

"I've no got a spade. I got my garden chipped ages ago, so I don't need to bother with all the shite. And, it's too late, you're no going haking about Gina's garden, she'll phone the polis, and that's the last thing we're needing right now."

"I have to. He said we have to do it tonight." Anna pleaded, folding the last toast in two and stuffing it in her mouth.

"He's no turning up here ten years late making demands on you. I'll go through him. Who does he think he is?" Christine pulls her tartan pajama bottoms up past her waist and tucks the shirttails in.

Anna looks at her with desperate eyes. Whatever Christine sees, it softens her.

"Tomorrow ok? We'll get you a spade, and we'll figure out a way to get Gina out of the house. Now, it's bed time. Your Dad was in the spare bed, but you can have it tonight. Watch your feet though, wee Alice is on the blow-up bed next to it."

"Do I have to share with her? Could she not go in your room?"

"Bed. Now."

Anna sighed, but was grateful for the warm bed upstairs, the toast in her belly, and for not having to dig after the night she'd had. Tomorrow was a better idea.

CHAPTER EIGHT

8

Anna

"Are you awake?" Christine asked, knocking gently. "Can I come in?"

"Oh my god, what the hell happened last night?" Anna groaned from face down on the pillow.

"Up you get, kettles on. She's been asking to come and wake you up since 7."

Anna looked down at the crumpled blanket on the floor bed beside her.

"Did you know about her?" She looked at Christine and rubbed her puffy eyes.

"I only found out about your sister when they appeared on the doorstep a couple of days ago."

"She's not my sister."

"Half-sister then, she's still blood."

"She's nothing to do with me."

"I know this is a lot to take in, but it's no the bairn's fault."

"It's his fault. He could of told me anytime in the last eight years. Do you think my mum knew he had another kid out there?"

"Your mum had a lot of questions about him. None of them were ever answered. She never knew where he was going, or if he was coming back."

"I thought he was dead, you know. I'd actually come to terms with never seeing him again."

"I think your mum was the same. Don't get me wrong, she had plenty of nights crying herself to sleep, but eventually, she got over him. She was moving on with her life."

"But do you think she knew about the money?"

"No way. She knew he got up to all sorts, but no chance did she know about that." Christine shook her head.

"We were sometimes so skint that we had no gas. Mum would turn the oven on and open the door. We'd sit in the kitchen and read books in our duvets because it was the only warm place in the house."

"There's no way she knew." Christine pointed down, out of the window into Gina's garden. "She'd have been out there digging it up with her bare hands, if she did."

"How are we going to get it?"

"I've not slept yet. I've been up all night thinking, and I've got an idea. If there's any money in the mud next door, we'll find it." Christine nodded in a knowing manner that always comforted Anna. However, she was a little apprehensive at what a sleep-deprived paranoid stoner might come up with to deal with this situation.

Christine bounced down the stairs and shouted back up,

"I've washed your clothes, hen. Put my dressing gown on and come down."

The fresh smell of bleached floors and tumble-dried washing wafted through the house. She took the stairs slowly, with each step thinking of how to greet them.

She walked into big smiles from Alice, a steaming cup of tea, and her entire outfit from yesterday folded into a clothes shop display style bundle.

"Morning, em... everyone." She pulled the dusky pink velour cord around her waist.

"So, what's the plans for today?"

"I've got an idea," Christine said, "I need to catch up on some sleep for an hour or two, so I thought a good plan would be for you two to go out for a wee quiet walk together."

"I'm not sure I've got time for that," Anna said, "I need to see Claire. She'll be wondering where I've got to."

"You've got plenty of time Anna. Take a quick walk up past the allotments. Yous can have a look around, see if there's anything interesting there."

Alice looked at Anna with hope in her big brown eyes.

"Don't we have more important things to be doing?" Anna drummed the table with her fingers and raised her eyebrows.

"There might be something at the allotments that you need?" Christine used her face to try and send a subtle message, but Anna wasn't picking up.

"Are we getting a shovel to dig up the money now?" Alice asked with a smile and a white milk mustache.

Anna and Christine looked at her, then each other.

"Did your dad tell you about that? Christ, he's nae shame that man." Christine said.

"Yeah, that's why we came here. To get the money for me and my big sister." She tried to catch Anna's eye, but she wouldn't respond.

"Ok darling, that's right." Christine opened the biscuit barrel, sat on the stool, and slid two chocolate digestives towards Alice. "So. How much money did he say was there?" She asked with a sweet tone Anna had never heard before.

"A thousand. Or a hundred thousand. Or a thousand hundred. Or a hundred. Something like that."

"Right, that's good. And, did he happen to say where he got it from?"

She crunched thoughtfully on a mouthful, tilted her head to the side, and said, "I think he said it was something complicated," as crumbs rolled down her t-shirt.

Claire

"You know that thing you told me last

night?" Claire whispered as the kettle boiled.

"About Shaun?" Irene came over to her shoulder.

Claire nodded, putting her finger to her mouth.

"We can't tell anyone. It would make me a suspect. It would complicate things."

"No one knows—only me and you. I couldn't tell anyone. I didn't know what had happened. For all I knew, It was you that killed him, and I wasn't going to get you in any trouble."

"But it wasn't me," Claire snapped, "I wasn't even there. I told you already."

Irene patted Claire's shoulder, "I know darling, I'm just saying, I didn't know, so I didn't risk it by telling anyone. And I never will."

"What about Jean? Does she know?"

Irene shook her head and leaned in a little closer, "The state she was in about the whole thing, about losing her car and you moving away, I couldn't tell her. I had to see you first, to find out what had happened."

The kettle steam rose between them, and the noise reached its peak.

"Let's keep it between us, please."

Irene nodded. "I promise, but please, tell

me something. Did you ever meet him? Do you know anything about him?"

Claire took a deep breath, buying a few seconds to come up with her answer. The first and only time she'd been in his company, she'd killed him. But, she couldn't mention that. All she knew was Anna's stories.

"I didn't meet him, I'm glad. He sounded horrible from what Anna said. He was creepy and aggressive, and..."

"Anna knew him? What did she have to do with him?" Irene's intense eyes burned into Claire as she stirred her tea. Sweat gathered between her breasts, and she blew the fine hairs up from her face as she juggled with possible answers in her head.

"Oh, I don't think she knew him personally, just knew of him. If you know what I mean."

Irene left a silent void, Claire's pulse throbbed in her ears. She couldn't say any more.

"So his death wasn't anything to do with you or Anna, just a weird random incident in your house?"

"Yep, really weird." She wiped her forehead with the back of her hand.

"Well, I'm glad. I'm glad he's dead, and I'm glad you heard what he was like from someone else other than me. I've fantasised so often about smashing his skull in to get back for what he did to me. It consumed me for years. What he tried to do to you, when you were growing inside me, I wanted to destroy him to protect you all these years. I wanted to protect you from him. Hide you in case he ever turned up, but I fucked it all up. I fucked up your childhood because of it. I'm so sorry."

"Why didn't you ever tell me any of this? I thought you just didn't like me." The lump in Claire's throat was impossible to swallow. She let it flow upwards into a stream of tears.

"Oh my darling, I'm so, so sorry," Irene wrapped her arms around Claire, the pink fluffy cardigan soaking up both their tears. "I love you so, so much, all I wanted to do was protect you, but I didn't know how, I didn't know where he was, so I just drank to block out the fear, then the paranoia was worse, so I took the tablets, then it all just spiraled. I've been pathetic, a terrible mother. I failed you so badly. My biggest fear took over, and I neglected you."

"Sometimes you couldn't even look at me. I thought you hated me." Claire said between sobs.

Irene wailed in pain, "I couldn't look at you because I was letting you down. I've spoken to so many therapists about it all. I've been coming to terms with my behaviors, it's been so hard, but then, when I heard his name on the radio, I felt a bit of hope. Then when I saw his face in the paper, I knew it was over, and it was time to make a mends with you."

Claire pulled away and dried her face with kitchen roll, handing another piece to her sobbing mother.

The door swung open, the handle hit the wall, and another little bit of plaster sprinkled the ground. One of the twins slid under the kitchen table meowing, followed by another, swinging a hoola hoop round above his head.

"Claire! Can we play Ker-plunk now?"

She sniffed, "Yeah, ok, go and set it up in the living room, and I'll be through in a minute. In fact, we both will. Me and my mum will be one team, and you two can be the other." She looked at Irene, who was still sobbing.

"Will you be on my team, mum?"

"Yes," she cried even harder, "I'd really like that."

Anna

"What's your favourite colour?" Alice asked.

"I don't know," Anna replied, walking quickly, trying to warm up and avoid questions.

"Is it blue? Mine is blue too. I think yours is blue because your bag and jeans are." Alice was skipping alongside Anna's purposeful steps. It reminded her of the way she walked, trying to keep up with Christine.

"Do you like hot or cold better?" She was getting out of breath.

"What do you mean? Hot or cold what?" Anna asked, irritated.

"The weather, like summer or winter, sunny or snowy."

"Hot, sunny, and summer. But unfortunately, I'm here instead, in the cold, crap winter."

"Well I'm glad I'm here. I don't like living

in hot places. It's boring."

Anna slowed down, feeling guilty for making her struggle, and very interested in her last statement.

"Really? Where did you live?"

"Me and Dad lived in lots of places. Sometimes I don't know what it's called, then we just stay there for a while, then go to another place."

"You know I've never even been to another country? I've never been somewhere hot, but he's taken you around the world by the sound of it. Lovely."

"Maybe we'll have time to go together. Maybe Dad will be able to take us both somewhere sunny. I'd like that, would you?"

"Na, I'm a bit busy for holidays right now. I've got a job back home and things to do."

"What job do you have? I want to be a chef when I grow up."

"I'm a waitress, well I was, I probably still am; actually it's complicated."

Alice laughed, "Adult stuff is always complicated."

The gate to the allotments was padlocked. They followed the wall to find a way in. Anna found an old half bag of cement that had got wet and was now solid. She rolled it up to the wall and used it as a step up.

"Wait here. I'll be two minutes."

"Wait, no, I'm not allowed to be myself anywhere. Dad will go crazy, I can't stay here alone. I have to come with you." She looked scared, her big brown eyes magnified with fear.

"Ok," Anna sighed, "I'll put you over first, swing your legs down and just drop. It's not that high."

She could feel her little hands shaking as she lowered her down over the wall. "It's ok, just jump." She let go and wailed. "Oooowww, my ankle, oooooowww." Anna climbed over and dropped down beside her.

"Sshhh, you don't want us to get caught breaking into an allotment, do you?" she crouched at her level and inspected her ankle. "It's fine. It's not broken, come on." She pulled her up by the hand, then walked slowly beside her, trying not to laugh at her excessive fake limp.

"Ow, ow, ow," Alice moaned quietly on every step.

"There, that's exactly what we need." Anna pointed to a wooden-handled spade resting against a wheelbarrow.

With the tool in hand, they headed back to the wall, Alice still limping badly, but now on the other foot.

"I'll go first this time, and I'll pull you over, ok?" Anna suggested. She lowered the spade down, then herself, then reached back over. As she dragged her up, Alice's arms tightened around her neck, and their cheeks touched. Her little face was soft.

"I think my foot might be broken. I don't think I can manage walking all the way back." She sat down on the hard mud, rubbing her ankle.

"I'm guessing you want me to carry you?" Anna asked.

"Yeah, please." She sprung to her feet and clambered onto her back. Anna threaded her arms under her knees. She picked up the spade and set off. Alice swung her legs happily and asked a string of 'what's your favourite' questions. Anna had never been asked most of these things, so it was kind of nice to have someone interested in her opinion on such a level. Although still definitely very annoying.

CHAPTER NINE

9

Frankie

"I hate fucking hospitals," Billy said.

"Everyone hates hospitals, here, put that gaffer tape in your pocket. Mine are stuffed already." Frankie turned the engine off and buttoned up his coat, "So, run this by me again. How do you think we're going to get him out of a crowded hospital during the day without causing a scene?"

"With this," Billy flipped open his jacket, flashing the gun and extra bullets, "We'll get him in a wheelchair and just walk out of there like we're taking our dear brother for a nice walk. He knows the script, and he certainly doesn't want any police attention.

Once he sees the gun, he'll cooperate."

"I hope you're right, and this doesn't turn into a nightmare in there."

"I really fucking hope so too, because if I have to drink much more of this poor excuse for coffee, I won't be held accountable for my actions." He poured the contents out of the window and tossed the empty paper cup into the back seat, on top of the growing pile of sandwich boxes, paper bags, and takeaway cups.

Frankie looked behind and shook his head, "You are a fucking animal, do you know that? I hate to think what your house looks like."

Tina & Maria

Tina and Maria's caravan wobbles with the hard knock on the door. Maria wraps the duvet round her and peers out the door.

"Get dressed you two. You've got work to do." Uncle James was on their metal step.

"Eh? It's too early. We don't have

anything to do. What are you talking about." Tina mumbled and pulled the covers over her head.

"You want me to keep quiet about the poor orphans? You get up and do what I say. I'll be back in ten minutes to pick you up. Make it snappy."

Maria groaned and slammed the door, "What the hell have we got ourselves into?"

Ten minutes later, they sat outside on a frosty bench, in tracksuits, with their hair pulled tight, rubbing sleep out of their eyes.

"Why did you even tell him? Ronin told us not to, and now he's going to use it forever. I don't want to be Uncle James's slave. What if he makes us climb on a roof or something?"

"I had to do something. I didn't see you helping; you were just greeting."

"No wonder, look at this." She unzipped her top and moved the t-shirt neck to reveal dark purple bruising, round painful marks where his fingers and thumb had been.

They sat as silent passengers, their breath visible inside the car, dreading whatever 'work' he had lined up for them. Just as the car's temperature was rising, they pulled into the hospital car park.

"What are we doing here?"

"You two are going to put your fine bull-shitting skills to the test."

"What do you mean?"

"You girls are fine actresses, now's your chance to shine. You go in there, say you're visitors for Andy McVay. You find out what bed and what room he's in, and tell him we said hello. That's it. Think you can manage that?"

"What do we say?" Maria asked.

"Whatever you like, you're his daughters, his girlfriends, whatever. The lies are your department, just get me the information. I'll be waiting here."

Maria held onto Tina's arm as they carefully walked across the icy car park. As they passed the blue Escort, Tina asked,

"Is that Ronin's old car? That English guy was quite hot. For an old guy anyway. I wouldn't mind getting a lift in that old banger," she giggled.

"Aw don't, that's the last thing we need. Come on, we're in enough bother already."

Tina puts on her poshest voice at the reception desk, using the lessons she's learned from mimicking Hillary. Maria bites her lip to stop a giggle from escaping.

"Hello, I'm wondering if you could help us? We need to visit our fatha. He's called Mr McVay."

"Can I have your names please?"

"Um, yes. I'm Anna of course, and this is my sis... erm friend I mean, I say sister, but we are actually friends."

"Uh hu, ok. Have a seat, and someone will show you up in just a sec. You might have to wait a while as it's only 2 per bed and his brothers went up a little while ago."

"That was terrible acting," Maria said from the side of her mouth as they took chairs in the waiting room. Tina was next to the children's toy area. She started spinning the coloured wooden beads over their metal wires from side to side. They flicked through the pages of dogeared magazines while slouching further into the chairs, till eventually, the receptionist approached them.

"I must apologise, there seems to have been a breakdown in communication somewhere. Your father's not in his room. He may be in another part of the hospital for treatment and it hasn't been recorded, or there's a chance he's left the building as none of the nurses seem to know anything."

"Aw well, it doesnae matter anyway," Tina said, in her regular voice to the puzzlement of the reception.

"Well?" Uncle James asked back in the car.

"She wouldn't take us up, said he's away for treatment or he's just away. She didn't know which, but they can't find him." Tina said while holding her hands over the heater vents.

"Sneaky fucking rat," James growled.

Jackson

"We've got two pies to keep our fingers in today Jamie. I'm going to need you to be vigilant."

"Yes, sir," he saluted her, "which pie is first?" He sucked his lips in, expecting a reprimanding, she ignored him.

"We need to try and find out names from last night. It will be tricky, always is with

Dougherty's. But, we need to speak to Anna, and hopefully catch up with Andy too since he disappeared before we got to the hospital."

"Right, shall we go to that house first then?"

"Yes, then we get straight back and get changed into plain clothes, then back on the trail of the others."

They pulled the unmarked silver Astra in five doors up from Christine's,

"Do you think there's a connection between the guy in the hospital and the guys from Swindon?" Jamie asked.

"No, just a coincidence. You know what they say, it's like waiting for a bus. You wait months for a case, then two come along at once." She angled her hat just right, and patted her notebook and pen.

"So you don't think it's funny that they just slowed down passing the same house we're going to?"

"What?" Jackson had been too busy imagining what she'd tell the Sergeant when she brought the Swindon guys in to spot them passing. "Are you sure?"

"Uh hu, look, both their heads turned. If they weren't looking for him, it would be an awfy coincidence, would it not?"

"No, I can't see it. What would they want with a dried-up old has been like him? He's just back to see his daughter, and the gypsies happened to catch up with him. Those guys are something else entirely." She said as she turned the keys.

"This can wait. Our targets are on the move! We can't follow them dressed like this! We need to get back and change right now."

"You could start by taking your hat off!" Jamie was already stripped down to his white vest, with his red scarf wound around his neck. Jackson chucked her hat in the back and pulled one arm out of her coat at the junction. She undid the seat belt, feeling guilty for breaking the law, and wrestled her other arm out of the sleeve, her elbow hitting the steering wheel and blasting the horn.

"Nothing like being discreet, eh?" Jamie said, shaking his head.

"Me? You're the one dressed like Freddy fucking mercury! Put your shirt on you idiot."

Hillary

Her old life had been comfortable, but now she realised, also incredibly boring. The most exciting plans she used to make were dinner arrangements or occasionally a day out with some friends. Now, she had to come up with ideas to trick people, outwit them and get the upper hand. The sun was coming up, but it was freezing in the van. She stripped her nightie off and pushed her bare breasts on Ronin's back. She stroked his thigh, and pushed her hips into his. He stirred and reached a hand behind, he pulled her closer. Finally, she'd get some relief, the tension had been building for days, and the excitement of all the drama made it worse. She needed to feel him now more than ever. He turned clumsily, eyes still closed, and wrapped his fingers in her hair. He spread her legs and climbed on top, no warm-up, no foreplay, just eleven hard thrusts, and a final grunt.

He rolled off, got up, and ran the tap to wash his face. She lay there fizzing with passion turning to poison, left to fizzle out in the cold bed. She needed to do something about this. This would not do at all.

CHAPTER TEN

10

Claire

"Here, look what I found in my wardrobe," Jean placed a Clark's shoebox full of photos on the table between Irene and Claire." There's some beauties in there." She handed them each a small pile, and began flicking through her own selection.

"How old are you in this?" Irene held out a picture of Claire and Anna dressed in bin-bags and red lipstick, with glittery green eyeshadow. Claire held it close to examine it. The dresses were held together with sticky tape, and they'd even taped black plastic bin bags up their legs into knee-high boots.

"We were 14. We dressed up as witches for the school Halloween disco. Other girls had shop-bought costumes or fancy complicated ones their parents had spent weeks on. All we had was a roll of bin bags and sellotape that Anna nicked from Roy's spar. We did look pretty good though." Claire laughed.

"I mind yous went trick or treating trying to get money for drink to take to the disco. All you got was a bag full of monkey nuts and fun size mars bars."

"We managed to get some wine though. We waited till Anna's mum answered the door to some kids and stole a rank bottle of red wine from her cupboard. Do you remember Debbie only used to give out raisins and dried apricots instead of sweets to guisers?"

Irene's bottom lip trembles, "I don't even remember any of that." Her eyes fill with tears as she stared at the image. Jean rubs her back, looking at Claire with a look that says, 'I should have known this was a bad idea.'

"Don't be daft Mum. I can't remember half of this stuff. Can you, Jean?"

"Nope, that's the point of photos isn't it?

To catch the things you forget. Don't feel bad."

"Here, look at this of you at the duck pond, and look at my perm! I cannae even remember that. Can you Claire?"

She did, vividly. And she knew Jean did too. They'd taken the boys down there last spring and told them about the day in the photo. Claire had been their age. She'd thrown half a loaf in the water and laughed as the ducks splashed and fought over it. Her mum had sat on a bench behind. There, but never present. The picnic had ended shortly after the photo when a huge seagull had shat all down the side of Claire's face and the shoulder of her pretty white dress.

"No, I can't remember either." She lied. They awkwardly brushed off and lied about a few more photos before being interrupted by a cat meowing under the table. Claire made a puzzled face to Jean, then looked down to see one of the twins on his hands and knees rubbing himself on the table leg.

"Aw, hello, are you playing at being a little cat?" Claire asked, getting a fierce hissed reply. The other twin skidded into the room with muddy feet and a stick in his hand, "Let's go! Harvey's coming!" he shouted, whipping the boy-cat under the table, who screamed and chased him, still on all fours.

"This is their new favourite game - Sabrina the teenage witch. Kyle is always Sabrina, and Connor gets to be Salem, which involves meowing and getting hit with a stick."

As they laugh, Claire takes the opportunity to close the photo box and put it in the airing cupboard. Having her mum be so sensitive was completely new for her. In the past she just got angry or disappeared. This emerging soft side was tricky to handle. She sat on the stairs, between the chatter in the kitchen and the screaming from the boy's room. Every time she was alone, even for a few seconds, she was back in her old living room, kneeling in the darkness, watching the blood and life leak from Shaun's head. Her father's head. She squeezed her eyes shut and wiggled her toes. Since that night, she'd often caught the smell of blood at unexpected moments, she knew it was her mind playing tricks, but in those moments, she was transported straight back there. Now, knowing the truth, those moments were becoming more potent and harder to shake herself out of.

She wanted to go home, to wash all her clothes, fold everything up and put them away in cupboards. She wanted to sleep in her own bed and get up with her own alarm. She wanted her and Anna safe inside watching something easy on the TV. She stretched her back and rolled her neck, then put on a cheery face as she entered the kitchen.

"Our train leaves quite soon. I need to go get hold of Anna."

"Can't you stay? I'm going back to the hospital tomorrow, can't you stay an extra night? I feel like I've just found you again, please?"

These were the kind of words she'd wished for all those years, through the shouting, the silence, and absence. Her mind said 'No, get the train!' but her heart couldn't resist.

"I could ask, I'll need to see what Anna's doing, but we probably could stay, just tonight. Would that be ok, Jean?"

"Of course it would. Gee her a wee phone and see."

Claire had never been more aware of the conflicting wants inside her. Her head was spinning - go home - stay here - it's safe - it's dangerous - go home - stay here - she felt dizzy - it was getting too much.

"I'll just go and see her quickly. I should see how things are going with her Dad anyway. I won't be long."

Her mind became still when the cold morning air hit her lungs. She marched with her hands in her pockets. It's ok, she thought; one more night will be fine, no one's looking for me, and I can handle my mum for a few more hours.

Hillary

"Ronin, come here, my darling. I've been thinking, we need to change tactics. None of Andy McVay's lot are going to hand him over. They are all as dodgy as they come. They know people are looking for them clearly. It's not going to be as easy as simply snatching him off the street. We need to be clever about it."

"I've got to be the one that finds him. I need to make sure I'm the one that avenges my Grandad."

"And let us not forget about the small issue of Anna McVay stealing all our money, yes?"

His angry lip curl signaled he was in just the right malleable state; he'd agree to most things if he was worked up enough.

"She made you look like such a mug. It's so unfair. I mean, you're not a mug at all, are you?"

"Am I hell. I'll show her, I'll take it out on her neck, and I'll rip her Dad's jaw, and I'll do it in my Grandad's name."

"Good, that's the Ronin I know. So, what we need to do is move our attention, from them directly, to the two blokes that bought your old car. They know more than us, and we need to find out what that is."

"Eh, aye, that was my next idea anyway." He agreed, easily.

"Did they say where they were staying? We need to be quick if we're to find them."

"No, they didn't tell me, but we'll easily spot that car a mile off. Come on, let's go for a drive around and look."

"Good idea. I knew you'd come up with a great plan. You always do." She said as she slipped on her grey cashmere gloves.

In the van, she pulled her beret down as far as it would go and her scarf as high as it would reach, so only her eyes were showing.

"What are you doing, woman?" Ronin asked as they spluttered out of the junction.

"I'm staying low profile. We can't be seen together, not if your plan's going to work."

"My plan? Right, aye." He agreed, and she smiled underneath the scarf, knowing he had no idea what was going on.

It wasn't long before they spotted the blue escort parked outside the Ashvale B and B.

"There it is. There they are!" Ronin shouted while bouncing and pulling his ear.

Hillary tutted. "When are you going to give up the god-forsaken ear tugging? You look like an imbecile!"

"Shut up woman, what will we do now?" He was far too over-excited.

"Just drive past, don't look!" she snapped. She bit her lip as she watched them get out of the car, swinging duffel bags over their big strong shoulders. She could tell their coats were expensive. The bald one caught her eye especially.

"We'll let them get in and settled. Then I'll approach them alone, soon. I'll find out what I can, and then we figure out the next course of action."

Hillary

"You remember what to say?" Ronin asked.

"I'm not a bloody simpleton. I can form coherent sentences without your help."

Hillary had backcombed her fringe extra high, and used the last of her special perfume. She'd been saving it for a special occasion, and this was definitely it.

She wasn't sure what she was dealing with; this was no thug, and certainly not a dull academic. He was something in between that she'd never experienced before. Whatever the outcome, this would be fun.

She pulled on her suede jacket. It had always been a little tight around the shoulders, but she'd unintentionally lost a few pounds—no more real butter, or cream in her coffee, no nightly Baileys or croissants for brunch.

"Park up the top of the corner, and I'll walk the rest; we don't want to be seen together."

"I'll wait here for you. You be careful now; these boys are dangerous."

"Don't wait, just drive home. I'll walk and meet you back there."

Once the van had spluttered out of sight, she checked her breath on her hand, puffed her hair up a little and made her way into the Ashvale B and B.

Hillary

It looked like her grandmother had been in charge of the interior design. A china vase with a king Charles spaniel painted on it, filled with plastic gladioli, sat on a crochet doily on the dark wooden table. It smelled of Vanderbilt perfume and dust. A little brass bell rang overhead, drawing the attention of a woman with floury hands wearing an apron.

"Hello dear, would you like a room?"

"Actually, I'm here for a business meeting."

"Are you? And who would that be with?"

"Um, I'm not sure of their names unfortunately. I was just sent to meet two

English gentlemen about their finances."

"Ooh, I know just the chaps. Who shall I say is here?"

"Just let them know that someone from McVay's finance is here, they'll know what you're talking about I'm sure."

"Okie doke, wont be long. Why don't you have a seat there?" She pointed at a wicker sofa with flowery frilly cushions. Hillary declined - she stood, carefully correcting her posture at the foot of the stairs.

Frankie

Ring Ring, Ring ring.

"I am not answering that. We should of been on the way home by now with her money, and the rest sorted." Billy said.

"I'll answer it then," Frankie reached for the phone. "She's not that unreasonable; she'll understand there's been a delay."

"Don't you dare," he swiped the phone

away, threw it in the bedside drawer next to the unread bible and slammed it shut. "You seem to have forgotten who you're working for, mate. She's worse than unreasonable. Remember Brighton? Or what she made us do to that guy in Soho?"

Frankie shuddered, "yeah, point taken. So let's get moving then. He's done a runner from the hospital, so..."

"So, let's check back at that house. Let's just kick the fucking door in and shoot him." Billy said.

"We need to find that money. And we ain't going to find the money if he's dead first."

"Ok, we force him to hand it over, then we finish them both off."

"I wouldn't have taken this contract if I knew there was a kid involved." Frankie rubbed his temple.

"A job's a job, and we're in too deep now. I am not going home empty-handed. We'll never get another contract again. We'll be blackballed. Do you want to go back to working the doors for peanuts?"

"I don't know. Would it be that bad?"

Billy shook his head in disgust, "Get your stuff together, we're going up to that house, and we aren't leaving till the job's done." He said, pushing a big roll of silver gaffer tape into one inside pocket and folding a flour sack into the other.

Knock knock,

Billy pulled the duvet over the gun and sat on top of it, "Come in," he shouted.

"Gentlemen, you have a visitor. A business meeting with McVay finance. She says you're expecting her. She's waiting in the lobby."

They look at each other, Billy shrugs.

"Of course, how could I have forgotten. Can you tell her I'll be right down?" Frankie smiles.

"What are you.." Billy started, Frankie quickly interrupted him.

"You stay here and prepare the paperwork," he pointed to the gun under the covers with his eyes, "and I'll go and introduce myself."

"Paperwork, right," Billy replied.

"Would you like me to arrange a table in the dining area for your meeting?" The woman asked.

"Yes, please." Frankie ushered her out and closed the door of the bedroom.

"What the fuck is going on here? McVay

finance, he's got a fucking nerve, I'm going down there..." Billy picked the gun up, the vein on his neck throbbed.

"No. I'll handle this. They obviously think they're being smart. So, we play them at whatever stupid game this is. Give me the gun." Frankie held his hand out.

"I'm coming with you."

"No. Just stay here. Whoever he's sent to do his dirty work is female; we don't want to intimidate her. I'll deal with this."

"Don't get taken for a mug down there. McVay would sail his own Gran down the river, remember that."

"Give me it," Frankie snatched the gun from Billy's hand, "I'm no mug. This is getting sorted, today. One way or another."

As he descended the stairs, she came into view from the feet up. Tight jeans, nice hips, blouse open far enough to show some cleavage, pink lips, nice big hair. He approached her slowly, looking her up and down, with one hand firmly holding the gun inside his coat.

"Alright darling, how can I help you?"

"Well, I think we may just be able to help each other." She smiled and offered him a hand.

CHAPTER ELEVEN

11

Hillary

"You're going to need a gun. You can get one, right?"

"Holy mother! What the hell have we got into here?" Ronin's jaw drops open.

"There's a lot of money involved, and I say it's ours for the taking. We just need to move first."

"What did they say? You've been away for ages."

"They didn't reveal much at all, just that they are here to retrieve a large sum of money, and our man Andy knows where it is."

"They must of said more than that; what

took you so long?"

"I had to make small talk first. I couldn't very well just demand to know their intentions, could I?"

"How do you know he's got a gun?" Ronin was pulling his ear so hard the skin cracked.

"I saw it obviously. I don't think he meant to show me, but his coat was open, and it was there, in the inside pocket. You can get a gun, can't you?"

"Uh, I think so. James and the other James have them for shooting deer. Will that do?"

"I'm sure that will suffice, yes. We need it immediately though. There's no time to waste."

"Hillary, I'm not sure about this. What do we do when we have the money? Won't those guys be after us? I don't want to be watching my back for bullets the rest of my days."

"Darling," she stroked the side of his face, "this is our opportunity to get out of that tiny van, and for you to get the respect you deserve. Those guys don't know anything about you or your family. We get McVay and turn him over, then use the money to benefit us. Once they know you're no pushover, they won't hang around."

"But they've got guns! In the name of god, woman!"

"And so will you. They won't have the balls to shoot anyone. It's all for show, I guarantee you. They probably don't even have bullets." She patted his knee and gave him her most reassuring smile. "They aren't a patch on you."

"I don't know about this. What if we're out of our depth? We don't know what any of them are capable of."

"And they don't know what you are capable of. I know what kind of man you are, and it's time the world got to see. Don't you think?"

"Aye, you're right. I'll do whatever it takes to get McVay and keep you happy."

"Goody. Now, we need leverage. They have two things we want, but we have nothing they want. We need to even it up a bit."

Claire

The cold walk has done Claire good; when she's moving, her mind's easier to control. She counts steps and red doors, lamp posts and drain covers. It stops her picturing that night, his body and the guilt dripping from her skin.

When cars drive by, she has to concentrate harder and count things faster to avoid the thoughts of being stopped by the police. Once that thought is triggered, within two seconds, her mind already has her up in court, found guilty for murder, plastered over the front pages of all the newspapers, and doing 14 years in jail.

She shook the thought from her head, entered the park and looked at the path ahead—just another few minutes to Christine's.

The grass was dull and patchy, nothing like the lush green they'd left behind in the summer. The trees stretched gnarly fingers above. As the wind picked up an empty tin can rolled across her path. She jumped, and put her hand on her thumping chest. "Jesus Christ, get a grip." She chastised herself for being so tense. She doubled her pace now the street was in sight, her temperature was rising, and her palms sweating. Her forehead was itchy with sweat under her woolly hat, but she couldn't slow down; she had to get out of sight.

She imagined there being no answer, having to go all the way back alone, heart pounding.

"Please, please, please, be in," she whispered as she stood between two cars preparing to cross the road, she couldn't hear properly for the wind, she quickly looked up and down, then ran, with her hands holding her hat down over her ears. Christine's was in sight now, only a few more meters to the gate. Once she was with Anna, she'd feel safe again. As she opened the gate, she saw the light on in the hall. With relief, she took the first two steps at once; then she couldn't go any further. Something stopped her from behind. She couldn't see. Her face was hot. Her knees buckled, her arms pulled at the shoulders, pain scared through her twisting wrists. The backs of her ankles dragged. Muffled scrapes and grunts, then tape stretching, winding. She's thrown onto cold metal, her arms tied behind her back, her breath damp inside the cloth covering her face, then it's dark. A metal door slams, then another, the engine starts, and she's moving. Sickness surges up her throat, wheels spin as they take off, she slides forward, bumping her head as the vehicle breaks suddenly. It's getting fuzzy; her ears feel like she's under water, she's no idea what's happening...

Christine

Christine's not used to sharing her home; she feels like there's crumbs everywhere. Everywhere Anna's been, and everywhere Alice's been. She should have slept while they were out at the allotment, but the feeling that those pikeys were in her house made her skin crawl. She'd hoovered twice already, but it wasn't enough. She ran the tap, testing it with her fingers. It wasn't hot enough, so she added a boiled kettle full. She got her favourite hard bristle brush and a handful of soda crystals. As the steam rose, she stared unfocused at the foggy kitchen window.

Two days ago, her life was empty, and just fine. Now it was full, of people and trouble and mess. And she was enjoying it. She thought back to being Anna's age, living on the edge, always having some drama to figure out or hide from. Those days were long gone, but now she felt more alive than she had for years.

She sloshed the hot bubbly bucket into the hall and got down on her knees. She scrubbed till a patch of white foam grew from the carpet. Her knuckles hurt, she was exhausted, she switched hands from one to the other. She was relieved to hear the knock on the door announcing Anna and Alice's return, she wanted them safe inside, and she was too tired to finish the floor. She slowly creaked and unfolded to a semi-standing position, with her hands on her thighs. "Hold on, I'm just coming," she shouted.

She moved her hands to the base of her back and stretched up further; she needed a joint. As soon as the bairns were in and cozy, she'd roll a wee medicinal smoke to soothe her muscles and her mind.

When she opened the door, a bandaged Andy pushed past her and went straight for the cupboard under the stairs.

"Out you come, dad's here. It's ok." He called into the darkness.

"She's out with Anna. Look, you've got some explaining to do, pal. You sent Anna back here last night to dig up Gina's garden all by herself in the middle of the night! What the hell are you playing at?"

"Out? Jesus, where?"

"Anna'll look after her, and they've not gone far."

"Jesus, Chris," he coughed, his face bright red, eyelashes sticking together with watering eyes, he thumped his chest, "she's not allowed out on her own. It's too dangerous out there."

"Calm yourself Andy. They'll be fine, sit doon, before you fall doon."

"I can't. I need to find them," he staggered toward the door, still coughing. Christine overtook him and slammed the door before he got to it.

"You're not going anywhere till you tell me exactly what's going on here. You cant bring this shit to my door and not tell me what's going on."

He looked at the ground, breathing deep and slow, shaking and weak. He rubbed his head, then lowered himself onto the bottom step of the stairs. He put his head in his hands and shook it.

"Oh, Chris, where do I start?"

Anna

"I'm quite hungry, you know," Alice tells

Anna as they pass Roy's Spar.

"You just had breakfast, didn't you?" Anna replied as she hoisted her up higher onto her back. She was light, but she'd been carrying her since the allotments, and it was starting to be a pain.

"Not that kind of hungry. More like hungry for a sweet."

Anna laughed; she knew exactly the kind of hungry she meant.

"Ok, jump down, and you can get something in here." As they entered, the old stale mop smell filled Anna's nose and she immediately felt Roy's eyes on the side of her face.

"Pick one thing, I've not got much money on me, and nothing too crazy. I don't want you getting all hyperactive." Alice nodded while studying the rows of chocolate bars and chewy sweets.

The rest of the shelves were as sparse as ever. Tinned steak and kidney pies covered in dust, shriveled apples, boxes of cheesy pasta with bashed corners and sticky juice tins in the fridge. It wasn't on anymore, Roy was obviously relying on the winter temperatures to chill the drinks.

She remembered standing on that spot,

leaning on the fridge, with Ronin growling in her face, and she started to feel overwhelmed. She'd forgotten the urgency of staying hidden, distracted by Alice. She needed to refocus. Get them both back to Christine's as soon as possible.

"Come on, hurry up, just choose something and let's go."

"Can I have this?" Alice presented a fudge.

"Is that all? It's pretty small. You can have something bigger, but be quick."

"No, this is all I want." She looked up with her big brown eyes, and Anna shrugged.

"Suit yourself."

At the till, Roy looked them both up and down. Anna stared back at him, noticing new unruly eyebrow hairs protruding since she saw him last.

"Not seen you for a while. Where you been hiding?" He asked.

Anna didn't reply, just tapped her nose.

"Yeah, nosy!" Alice said, giggling, taking Anna's hand as they left the shop. She pulled her through the door, laughing.

"I see your ankles better now. Do you think you can walk back to Christine's?"

"Actually, it's still really sore, but..."

"Shit!" Anna dropped to her knees and spun Alice to face her.

"Pretend I'm tying your laces," she whispered urgently. Alice obeyed without question, presented her foot, and looked down onto Anna's head.

"Don't make it obvious, but tell me when that big blue van's gone past."

Alice bit open the end of her fudge and spat the wrapper onto the pavement, checking the road as she did, while presenting Anna the other shoe to pretend to tie.

"It's away now, went round that corner. Are you in trouble with them?"

Anna stood, wiped her knees, and let Alice jump up onto her back.

"Let's get to Christine's, put your hood up and hold on tight."

She giggled and bounced up and down like a jockey on Anna's back as they hurried along the road.

CHAPTER TWELVE

12

Claire

She can see little rectangles of blurry light. There's tape over her mouth; she expands her nostrils trying to get more air, a bubble of snot blows from her nose. Her eyes feel crusty. She's been unconscious, left face down on a bed. Her hands are taped together behind her. She tries to move, to peel them apart. Her skin stretches and nips with the glue. Steps approach. She stops moving, plays dead. The door opens a crack, the light changes, she senses two people come in.

She can hear girls whispering.

"You take it off."

"No, you can. I'm not touching her. What if she's dead."

"Hillary said just sit with her, keep her quiet for a few hours, and Ronin will give us a grand."

"Do you even know who it is?"

"No, that's why I want you to take the bag off."

"But she'll see our faces. What if she grasses."

"It can't be anyone from round here, or she wouldn't be making us do it."

They're almost inaudible, but Claire knows exactly who it is, and now she knows it was Ronin that dragged her from Christine's steps and into that van. The last time she'd seen him, he was on his knees in the garage forecourt with blood dripping from his hands. She'd spent the last six months worried about the police and feeling so guilty for what she'd done, the Dougherty's money had barely crossed her mind. How could she of thought they'd get away with it?

She started to wriggle, not too much, just enough to show she was conscious. She wanted this gag off, and she was ready to comply. Her time was up. Everything was catching up with her and she'd have to take the consequences.

"Shit, she's awake, go on, take the bag off."

"I can't, I feel sick."

"For fuck sake, I'll do it," Maria pulled the bag from the top, taking Claire's hat with it. The girls stood wide-eyed, silent.

Claire tried to look calm, hoping for the tape to be taken off. She badly wanted to wipe her face. Sweat and tears had stuck hair all over her face, and her nose ran down the edge of the tape.

"Fuck." Maria said.

"Should we take the tape off?" Tina whispered. Claire nodded, sending the please with her eyes.

Tina knelt beside her. " If I take it off, you can't scream, ok?"

Claire nodded again.

Hillary

"Let me have a look at it." Hillary holds her hands out, and Ronin places the wooden handled gun into them like it's a delicate newborn baby. She inspects it from all angles, polishes the barrel up with her sleeve.

"It's bloody ancient. It's like something a highwayman would use. Are you sure it works?"

"It's the only one that wasn't locked in the cabinet. We can just use it to scare them anyway, doesn't matter if it works or not."

"No, no, no. We need bullets, and clarification that it will fire if need be. Did you get bullets? For goodness sake, please tell me that you got bullets. What use is a gun with nothing to fire?"

Ronin searched his pockets. He produced an array of red, yellow and blue shotgun cartridges, some tiny lead slugs and six brass bullets. "That's all I could find."

"Ok, good, these look like the chaps." Hillary smiled as she rolled a brass tube between her finger and thumb. She unclipped the chamber easily and placed two bullets inside. She closed it and polished her finger prints off, then held it out for him. He hesitated, drawing his hand back.

"Does it really need to be loaded?"

"Yes, and we need to test it."

He held a shaking hand up, aiming towards the field beyond the site.

"Not here! Everyone will hear. Get in the

van. We'll get out of the town a bit to test it."

"What about..." he made a 'you know who' gesture towards the caravan where Claire was held.

"The girls are sitting with her. They'll keep her quiet."

"Lord give me strength! You got those two brats involved?"

"Excuse me? I'm doing the best I can with a very bad situation. You're the idiot that grabbed the wrong person!"

"At least I got someone! Anyway, the Mcvay's will still pay for her. That's Anna's wee side kick."

"Let's hope Andy McVay has a similar sentiment for the girl." Hillary looked at her watch. "We need to get going. The clock's ticking."

"What if she screams? I'll get murdered if my Ma finds out we've got someone tied up in there."

"Don't worry. I told you the girls have it under control."

"You can't trust that pair!"

"I told them you'd pay them handsomely for their help and loyalty."

"No fucking doubt, they always manage to get their sticky fingers on my cash."

"Don't be greedy. They are doing you a favour. And, apart from me, those two girls are the only people you can count on."

"Like I said, Lord, give me fucking strength."

"All of this will be done and dusted soon enough. Just stick to the plan. We nip out and make sure the gun works, then present our dear little hostage in return for all the money. In and out, before anyone else gets a look in."

Anna

They didn't need to knock. Christine was waiting with the door on the chain, watching the street. With Alice still clinging on like a baby koala bear, they were swallowed into the clean, warm air. She dropped the spade in the hall, then lowered Alice down onto the soft, and flopped beside her, panting.

"You are heavier than you look," Anna laughed, taking her coat off.

"Where the hell have you two been? We were worried seek." Christine said.

"We? Who's we? Did Claire come round?" Anna asks, still panting, as the noise of feet descending the stairs gets louder.

"Dad!" Alice shouts, runs and wraps her arms around his legs. He steadies himself on the wall, visibly frail and in pain.

"Girls, are you ok? You shouldn't have gone out. It's too dangerous just now."

Anna stays quiet, observing the affection between her father and his younger daughter. Jealousy grips her insides.

"We were getting a spade to dig for the money, and I broke my ankle, and we got a sweet from the shop."

Andy rubbed her head, smiling, "I see your ankle's better now, though."

"Yes, because my sister carried me all the way."

He looked at Anna and said, "Well, that's what big sisters are for." She looked away, refusing to acknowledge his words.

"So Christine," Anna started, "how are we going to get into Gina's garden without her seeing?"

"I've no been to my bed yet, I was going to, but then your Dad came in. Discharged himself from the hospital, didn't you Andy," Christine tries to bridge the tension. "I think there's only one thing I can do. I need to go roond there and make ma peace. I'll tell her some shite about the bingo. I've won free tickets, and I want to take her to make up for before. For giving her a hard time about Gizmo, god rest his fluffy wee soul. I'll tell her I'm taking her oot. It's on me."

"You think that will work? Won't she be suspicious?" Andy asked.

"She's a tight-fisted auld boot. I've seen her eating the peanuts oot the birdseed in the garden. She'll not say no to a free night at the bingo. I'll tell her there's a free drink in it too."

"How long will that give us," Anna asks.

"Couple of hours. I can get her oot by seven, so you'll have till the back of nine. Is that plenty?"

"It will need to be," Andy replied.

"So, where exactly is it? You can't just dig up her entire garden in a couple of hours in the dark, hoping to find it." Christine asked.

"He told me last night, sealed plastic tubes, two in the right corner by the window, two by the edge nearest the gate, and one right under the tree. Is that right?"

"I'll do it; now that I'm here," Andy said, still trying to catch her eye properly.

"Aye, make sure you're in the right place, there's no time for making mud-pies. In and out, quick sharp. And, mind you's cant be getting caught by the Dougherty's either."

"They'll think I'm still in the hospital, don't worry about them."

"Dad, what about..." Alice started. Andy patted her head.

"Nothing to worry about, darling."

"But the.."

"Nothing at all." He was squeezing her shoulder now, and she stopped talking.

"The police will be back too. They want to find out what happened last night." Anna said, wringing her hands.

"You can't tell them anything! No names, nothing, you can't mention me, or..."

"I'm not daft, Dad. I already told them I didn't see anything. I told them I just opened the door and saw you on the road. I don't know who they were, or what happened."

"Did they see Alice? Does anyone know she's here?"

"I'm not daft dad," Alice echoed her big sister, "I was in the cupboard till Anna came back, then we had ice-cream."

The relief on his face adds another jealous knot in Anna's stomach. He hadn't cared enough to send her as much as a postcard in a decade. Her eyes began to heat up with angry tears.

"Who wants a cup of tea?" she asked, heading for the kitchen quickly before anyone saw.

Christine didn't miss it though, she followed Anna through and put a warm hand on her arm.

"He's a tactless bastard, your dad. But, the bairns just wee, and he cares about you just the same."

Anna shakes her head, rubbing her eyes.

"What's going on, Christine? This is all crazy, a kid sister that hides in cupboards, my long-lost Dad that doesn't give a shit getting left for dead on the street by the Dougherty's, and now we've to search for buried fucking treasure. This is ridiculous. In fact, I'm going home. I'm going round to Jeans, and I'm getting Claire, and I'm going to the train station and forgetting any of this bullshit even happened." She zips up her coat and reaches for the door handle.

Christine takes both her hands and squeezes them. "You can't go yet; they need you. Andy needs to make it up to you. He's here to get you that money. And the bairn needs you, can you not see she dotes on you already? She's family."

"She's not. Neither of them are. I don't have a family. I don't need any of them." She's talking firm, but her eyes are streaming. Christine takes her in a hard hug and pats her shoulder. As Anna swallows the lump in her throat back down, a little hand tugs her sleeve.

"Do you like Twixes? Or Chewits?" She holds out a choice, but she doesn't reply. Christine takes the twix. "Thanks, darling, I happen to know Anna loves twixes. Here you go." She jabs it into Anna's hand, and she reluctantly accepts and peels the wrapper open.

"Did your Daddy bring those for you?" Christine asks.

"No, I got them from the shop me and Anna went to."

Anna laughs and coughs on the first bite.

"The shop we got the fudge from?"

"Yeah. I thought we might need sweets for later, so, you know, I just got them for us."

"Sit down Dad, you look terrible," his

cough was relentless, his knees were buckling under the force. Christine gave him a bottle of Benylin and a sympathetic smile. He opened the cap between coughs and drank half the bottle.

"You've no got the strength to be digging oot there in the freezing cold," Christine said.

"I'll be fine in a bit, once this stuff kicks in and I get some food down me later on."

Anna looked at his bandaged head and his shaking hand. He wasn't the dad she remembered from all those years ago. He could have dug all night in any temperature. He was strong and capable.

"I'll do it." Anna said, "You keep a lookout, and I'll dig. If anyone comes, I can run. You stay in here with the doors locked."

"I couldn't make you do that, my darling," he said, licking the sticky medicine from his lips.

"It's our only option, and if this money really exists, I want to find it."

"Don't you believe me?" Andy looked hurt, Alice looked up from her cross-legged position in front of the TV.

"I don't know; you don't really have the best track record. The last time I believed you was when you told me you'd see me soon - ten years ago." Anna watched the hurt and regret change his face a little.

"That's why we're here, to make it up, I know..."

"That's it settled then," Anna interrupted, uninterested in what was coming next, "I'll dig. You watch out of the window and alert me to anyone coming."

"I can dig too," Alice added.

"No, you're not going out there," Andy said.

"Can't I help digging? I'm good at digging." She moaned.

"I know what you can do." Anna asked, "Are you good at drawing?"

"Quite good. I drew a cat once, and it actually looked like a real one."

"You can draw the treasure map then, deal?" Anna offered her hand out and Alice was delighted to take it.

"From Christine's bedroom, you can see right into Gina's, you can draw it out and you put the X's on it." She said as she looked in the sideboard for pens and paper.

"Here you go, why don't you go up and get started," she passed an unused envelope to Alice, and she happily ran up the stairs.

She looked at her dad with his bandaged head and bruised face, resentment turning to pity, but still swimming in mistrust.

"This is fucking ridiculous. You do know that?"

"I, I know it's a bit far-fetched," he stammered.

"I need to ask, but I don't think I really want to know the answer. Where did the money even come from, if it exists?"

Andy sighed, "It's complicated..."

"Of course it is," Anna shook her head and went to help Alice with the map drawing.

"That was not easy. She's even tighter than I thought. I had to promise her two bingo books, three drinks, and a packet of Rothmans fags. I dunno who she thinks she is; it should be her apologising to me. Anyway, I'm calling for her at half six, so you'll have till the back of nine."

"We'll make it worth your while Chris, I owe you big time. Not just for this, for everything you've done for Anna."

"Dinnae you get all soppy. It doesn't suit you."

Alice shouts for Andy to help them upstairs. He takes them slowly, coughing and using the banister to pull himself up. Christine stayed close behind, ready to steady him if he swayed too far back.

Alice leans on the dressing table, chewing the end of a pink pen. The envelope has been elaborately decorated with daisies, toadstools, and a frog.

"That looks great, darling," Andy said; she beamed pride from her big brown eyes.

"Remember and draw the apple tree in the middle. That's the most important bit. Then show me where the gate is, and then draw in the path."

"You're a wee artist hen," Chritine said, "just like your big sister. She used to love drawing too."

"Can I open the blinds so we can get a better look?" Anna asked.

"Och, let me do it, you're no messing them up," Christine pushed her away from the cord, and carefully and evenly lifted them. All four of them peered down into the garden next door. Andy rubbed his chin and his brows knitted together in concentration. He held the map on the windowsill, turning it to fit the scene below. He drew five crosses, two in the left corner, two in the bottom right, and one under the apple tree.

"Right, I'm needing a lie down. I've still no been to ma bed, and if av to put up wee Gina tonight, I'm going to need some energy." Christine said as she slid the blinds back down.

"Girls, I could really do with a lie down too," Andy said, trying to hold in a cough and rubbing his head. Can you keep each other entertained downstairs for a couple of hours?"

Anna sighed, "Yeah, ok."

"Don't answer the door. We only need to get through a few hours. If you see any of those Dougherty's, you wake me up, ok? And Alice, you know what to do, don't you?"

"Yes, I'm not daft, dad."

CHAPTER THIRTEEN

13

Billy

"So it's definitely on for tonight?" Billy asks as they circle Christine's street again.

"Once it gets dark and the street quietens down. We get the job done, and get fuck out of here. We're not waiting and pussyfooting about anymore."

"Shouldn't we keep a low profile till then?"

"We are low profile. He don't know we're here. No one knows we're here."

"Apart from the pikey and his Mrs. You didn't tell her why we're here, did you?"

"Don't be fucking stupid, I told her he had our money, and we're taking it back, nothing else."

"Why did you tell her anything? I don't trust her. For all our sakes, I really hope you didn't run your mouth off."

"I didn't. Anyway, she's too classy to be involved with McVay."

"You reckon? What's she doing with that Gypsy then?"

"She's a proper lady. I'm telling you."

"Why's she shacked up with him then? Must like a bit of rough."

"Can we stop for some grub before we go back? I'm starving."

"Ah, look what we have here! Up at the window, the lot of them just standing there. Look! The kid, she's there," Frankie points, slowing down as they descend the hill.

"Is he there?"

"I think so; maybe, there's a few of them."

Billy pulls the gun out of his coat, unclips the seat belt and reaches for the door handle.

"Calm down! Put that away you animal! You can't go in there with a gun in broad daylight! Put that seat belt back on!" He speeds up to stop Billy from jumping out of the car, they look up again, and the blinds are closed.

"You need to get grip mate, take it easy.

Now we know for certain they're in there, we can wait it out. It'll be dark soon, then, and only then do we produce that fucking thing. Got it?" his face is red, his throat hurts from the sudden shouting.

Billy's polishing the gun on his knee with the lace doily, he doesn't look up, but mumbles "I'd take the lot of them out, in daylight, right now if it was up to me."

"You are a liability; you know that?"

"I'd knock on the door, get in there and hold them all up, put the gun to the kid's head and force him to hand over the goods. I don't know why you're hanging back."

"We don't know if he's even dug it up yet. It's buried, remember? He's the only one that knows where. Right now, we're going back to get some rest; I've got a feeling it's going to be a long night."

Hillary

Hillary picked up a faded old Irn Bru tin, wiped the moss from the side, and balanced it on top of a fence post. She walked the hundred yards back to Ronin's side, watching him fumble with the gun in shaking hands.

"Give it your best shot then." She put her hands over her ears and waited, braced for the noise.

He closed one eye, raised his hand, and waited. He dropped his hand, shook the tension from his shoulders, and tried again. He closed the other eye this time. His hand trembled.

"Give it here," she snapped, snatching the gun from him. She aimed and fired without hesitation. The shock took her breath away; she stared, unblinking at the space where the tin had stood and the hole in the tree far beyond. She blew a stream of air from her mouth, raised her eyebrows, and smiled.

"It works then."

"How?" Ronin asked, bouncing on his toes, "How did you hit that? Have you shot a gun before?"

"Of course I have. Haven't you?" she looked at him as if he'd said something disgusting. "Mummy and I used to go shooting all the time when I was young. I'm sure I told you."

"Well, well, the life of a posh girl, eh? Us poor kids are struck peeling tatties, and you're out there shooting up the woods." He looked her up and down; she could see the resentment.

"Yes, and it's just as well we aren't relying on your skills today, isn't it, darling?"

He muttered something under his breath as she tiptoed round the muddiest part of the path to inspect the hole she'd made in the tree.

"What was that? Something you want to say?" She shouted over her shoulder.

"Nope. Not a thing. Let's just get back and make sure those brats haven't stuck us in."

"We have a couple of hours before we can do anything tonight. Drop me off in town. I need to pick up a couple of things from the shops in preparation."

"Like what? I'll come with you."

"No. You don't need to go everywhere with me. It's women's things ok? Nothing to concern yourself with. Your priority is making sure no attention comes to your caravan before it gets dark."

Anna

Anna looks out of the peephole on the way past. The street is empty and dull, like nothing is going on. Just another boring day, but not for them. She's starting to feel nervous. She'd always wished for her Dad to come back and make her feel safe. This wasn't how it was meant to be.

She checked the back door and the windows, just like Christine always did. She picked up the phone and listened to the dial tone to make sure it was working. She decided to ring Jean's and make sure Claire was ok with staying another night.

"Aw hiya, hen. She's already on her way to you. She should be there by now. Maybe she's bumped into someone."

Anna gets an uneasy feeling, "Did she walk over?"

"Aye, between you and me, I think she was needing a break from her Mum. It's going as well as can be expected, but, well, she's kind of hard work."

"What time did she leave?"

"A wee while ago, I'm not sure exactly, she wanted to check it was fine to stay another night, I said I'm sure it would be, but she wanted to see how things were going with your Dad. How are things? I wasn't sure if I should phone when I saw him, but then I thought, if it was me, I would want to ken, so I thought..."

Anna's not listening. She knows it takes less than fifteen minutes to make that journey, and she knows Claire wouldn't be in the mood to stand chatting to anyone on the street.

"Right, I have to go, Jean, I'll see you later, yeah." She can still hear her rambling faintly as she replaces the receiver. She turns the TV down low, sits Alice in front of it with a bowl of crisps, and begins pacing between the front and back of the house. She wants to go out and search for her, but she can't leave the house. They are too vulnerable. She rolls a cigarette, sitting on the edge of the footstool by the window.

"I'm just going out the back to smoke this, ok?"

Alice nods without looking away from the TV. Sitting on the cold step, she lights it and inhales the warm smoke. It doesn't help much. She's trying to make some order out of whats going on. She tries to concentrate on making a list of things to do before they can find the money,

1, get spade, done,

2, get rid of Gina, done,

3, make a map, done,

4,

She can't think. She's too worried about Claire. The cigarettes gone out, and her fingers are numb. Maybe she went to the supermarket, or maybe she had to go up the High Street for something. Or maybe she's visiting someone on the way. None of these sounded right. She dropped the cigarette onto the little pile by the back door and started wringing her hands together; then there was a knock on the front door. She exhaled relief as if she'd been holding her breath for a very long time and ran to open it.

"Wait," Alice whispered as she slid past her and into the cupboard with her bowl of crisps.

Anna looked through the spy hole, smiling, expecting to see Claire, but it was someone else.

Frankie

Frankie lay on his back, with his fingers entwined across his chest. Billy's snoring from under the covers had started as a gentle purr, but was now rattling the lampshade. This always happened. If he didn't get to sleep first, he was doomed to listening to his piggy snorts and grunts for hours. He'd once woke him up with a gun to his head through lack of sleep, and all Billy had replied was 'put toilet roll in your ears.' He wasn't even phased with a death threat. He was unhinged. As soon as this job was done, he was cutting him loose. He'd take the payout and disappear. France maybe. He fancied spending a summer picking grapes. He'd thought about it years ago, but he'd got dragged into working and bills and rent, and never made it. But, maybe now was his chance. He tuned out the noise from the next bed, and imagined himself in a dusty vineyard, huge purple grapes hanging in front of him, the sun beating down on his back… then there was a quiet knock on the door. So quiet he couldn't tell if it was their door or another. He decided to ignore it and tried to sink back into his French daydream. The knock came louder this time, definitely on their door. He waited for Billy to respond, then shook his head and sighed. He wasn't going to get any sleep before tonight. He opened the door a little, just enough to see who was there. He stood up taller, and straightened his shirt.

"Well, nice to see you again, sweetheart. What can I do for you?" He asked, then slid out of the door and pulled it closed behind him.

CHAPTER FOURTEEN

14

Anna

"So what can you tell me about last night?" Jackson asked.

"I told you everything already. I've no idea what happened."

"Uh hu, so you said. And you reckon you've no idea who the men were who attacked your father?"

"No, no idea."

"What was your dad doing up here anyway? From what I've heard, he's been missing in action for quite a while."

"Aye, that's my dad. He's a tricky man to get hold of." Anna hears a crunch sound from the cupboard and coughs to try and covert it up.

Jackson tilts her head to the side and taps her pen on the notebook. "Where is he now then? He left the hospital in a hurry, forgot to leave his contact details. We really need to get hold of him, so..." she looked expectantly at Anna.

Jamie took a step closer to the cupboard, leaning his ear towards the faint rustling.

"He's gone home. He got out of the hospital and went home. But, I, I don't know where his home is." Anna stuttered, standing up to distract their attention.

"Hang on, Anna, we need to straighten this out. You came back here to see your dad. He was attacked, but you don't know why, or who by. Now he's gone, and you don't know where?"

Anna nodded, trying to portray a combination of concern and confusion, Jackson stared right back. She was giving nothing away. Anna had no idea if she was buying it or not.

"Well, that's about as far as we can go today then. Please, when you do find out where he is, pass on my details and ask him to get in touch." Jackson handed her a card.

Anna took it and pretended to read it

carefully to break away from her stare. She held the living room door open to guide them out. Relief flooded her chest as they both moved towards her. Then Jamie took a step back towards the cupboard door again, straining to hear.

"Mice." Anna said.

"Ew," Jamie's nose wrinkled up.

"In fact, I think it's rats. I saw one about this size earlier." She held out her hands about a foot apart.

"Ok, we're done here. We'll be in touch again Anna."

Jamie squeezed between them, through the door, and stood outside.

"Don't think this is over just yet." Jackson lingered in the doorway for a second too long, her eyes flicking to the top of the stairs.

Claire

"What are they planning to do with me?" Claire asked as Maria took the cigarette end out from between the fingers of her taped-together hands.

"I don't know. They never said, just said we have to keep you quiet till they get back."

"Hillary told me, It's to do with Anna's dad and grandad's money, I know that much," Tina added.

"Andy? Not me?" A strange surge of relief and anger burst through her chest and into her stomach.

"I don't think it was supposed to be you. I think he wanted to get Anna and use her to get the money back."

"Tina, will you shut up? We shouldn't be telling her any of this."

"Why? It's pretty obvious. And she'll soon see what's happening. They're going to have to swap her at some point."

"So it's not actually anything to do with me? I was just in the wrong place at the wrong time?" Claire felt the pain in her ankles where they'd been dragged along tarmac, the bruising down the left side of her body where she'd been thrown onto the metal, the ache in her arms and shoulders where they'd been wrenched behind, and the burning skin round her mouth where the tape had gagged her.

"Pretty much."

"Story of my bloody life," Claire lifted

both hands and sighed, "Any chance you can untie me then?" The fear of what was coming to her was fading away in the shadow of a burning sense of injustice.

"No way, Hillary will kill us."

"I didn't do anything when you cut the gag and let me sit up, did I? I'm not going to now. Please? My wrists are really sore." She sat up straighter, offering her hands out, trying to scan the caravan contents without making it obvious.

Tina finds the end of the tape and starts to unpick it.

"Wait, don't." Maria stopped her. "We've managed this far; just keep it on a bit longer. They'll be back soon."

Tina shrugs and mouths' sorry' as she lets Claire's wrists go, still tightly taped together. Maria sees the exchange.

"Look Tina, we are in enough bother this week. I can do without Ronin being on our case as well. Let's just do what we're supposed to, ok?"

"Whatever, I'm going along with it, I'm not fighting or struggling. I don't have the energy. I'll just wait till I get handed over later on."

"You're awfy relaxed for someone that's

been chucked in the back of a van with their mooth taped up."

Claire shuffled to the edge of the bed and put her feet on the floor, testing a little weight on her ankles. It was painful, but could probably take more.

"Sit back there," Maria points, instructing her back into position.

"Sorry, I just need to stretch a little bit." The telltale sweat was beading on her chest under her clothes, but it wasn't anxiety; it was adrenaline. She rolled her shoulders and tilted her neck from side to side, and made the right stretching noises, all the while taking inventory of her surroundings. The tiny sink, the single ringed hob; the frying pan; the steel kettle; the candle stub; the chemical toilet with a wonky hanging door, a glass ashtray, an enamel mug, an open carton of milk.

"Em, girls, I have to be honest here. I am bursting for the toilet. Can one of you untie my jeans?"

"I'm not. You'll have to do it, Tina."

"Aw, for fuck sake. Seriously, do I have to do everything?"

"Or you could just rip this tape off?" Her breathing quickened as the girls looked at each other, deciding if it was safe or not. "I'm really bursting, I don't think I can hold it much longer."

"Stand up. I'll pull your fucking jeans down." Maria snapped, holding her arms out, waiting for Claire to present her zip. She winced as her ankles took her full weight, but the adrenaline dulled the pain as the energy built up.

"Just untie her bloody hands for two minutes. She's not going anywhere." Tina interrupted the awkward advance.

"Fine, give me them. And don't you dare try anything."

"I told you, I don't have the energy to fight this. I'm just going to go along with whatever they want to do so I can get home." Claire smiled briefly, hoping to put them at ease, edging a little closer to the door. As Maria crouched and stripped away the first layer of tape, Claire took half a step backward toward the door, hoping it was undetected. She could feel Maria's eyes watching, from where she lay on the bed, examining every twitch of her face. Every blink under total scrutiny.

"Wait," Maria said, "don't take it off. We can't trust her. Come on, use your brain,

Tina."

Tina looked up, her face changing like a bad smell had just invaded her nostrils. She folded the bit of tape back down, as she began to stand, she lost her balance for a second and gripped Claire's wrists tight with one hand and steadied herself on the floor with the other. That little wobble was the chink in the amour. It had to be now; Claire had to move, tied or untied. She yanked her hands from Maria's grip and kicked her in the groin. Maria reached out with one hand like a claw, she crumbled to her knees and held between her legs with the other. She howled and swiped at Claire's leg. Tina sprung from the bed with crazed eyes and made a noise like a wolf stuck in a bear trap. Claire grabbed the frying pan from the hob and swung it like a pro golfer, her tied hands becoming an asset. As Tina got nearer, leaping across the tiny space, with Maria on the floor beneath, the steel struck her cheekbone. Claire saw her expression in slow motion; her jaw swung to the side, a string of saliva trailed through the air, her eye's rolled, her body softened, she landed on top of Tina, a mass of tangled limbs wedged in the three-foot space.

Claire fumbled with the lock, her double hands a hindrance once more; she pulled the silver latch and put all her weight on the door with her shoulder. It swung open into the cold, cloudy afternoon. She tumbled out onto the ground and scrambled to get to her feet. She had to move quick, she didn't need to figure anything else out; she just had to run. Her feet were getting traction. The icy wind blew the sticky strands of hair from her face. Her muscles were heating up, she was picking up speed and getting some distance, then she felt a searing pain from the back of her head. Her feet slid, her body was going forward, but her head was being yanked back by the hair. She lost her footing and slammed down hard. Her head bounced off the ground. Her eyes closed with the impact. When she opened them again, she could see up Ronin's nose and down the barrel of his gun. Above him, the sky was dark grey; around her, she could hear nothing but her own pulse.

Anna

"You can come out now," Anna whispered into the cupboard.

"Dad will go crazy if he knows the police were in here, I'm not allowed to talk to them, and he says they always try and trick you into getting into more trouble."

"Well, it's his fault they came. Look, I need to go out and find my friend, she should have been here by now. I'm worried something happened to her. I won't be long."

"Can I come?" her big brown eyes pleading.

"No, it's too dangerous, you stay here and watch the tv. Dad and Christine are upstairs; just shout them if you need anything. I'll be back soon."

"Pleeease? I'll be lonely and sad by myself. What if those bad guys come back? What if someone knocks on the door?"

"No, just stay here." Anna snapped. Alice's lip quivered, and she squeezed one hand in the other. She looked so small and innocent. Anna felt guilt in the pit of her stomach.

"Ok, ok, get ready quickly. I don't have

time to mess about. Get your coat and shoes on."

Alice put her hood over her head like a cape and hastily put her shoes on the wrong feet. Anna sighed and helped her into the coat properly and replaced the shoes correctly.

When they slowed down, catching their breath after running across the road, Anna asked,

"So, what did he do?"

"What did who do?" Alice replied as if she was waiting for the punchline of a joke.

"Our dad, what did he do that was so bad that you have to hide in cupboards?"

"It's just in case Angelica comes."

"Who's that then? Someone he owes money to?"

"No, it's just my mum."

Anna halted and spun her around by the shoulder,

"He's hiding you from your own mum? What the hell? He can't take a child from her mother, that's horrible. I can't believe this; he's worse than I though." Anna pinched the bridge of her nose, feeling her pulse thump in her head.

"It's ok. She doesn't like me anyway. She always shouts at me and says, "You're just like your father!" She does an impression, wagging her finger and making a face of disgust.

"But she's looking for you. Of course she likes you. She's your mum."

"No, she doesn't. She says she can't even look at me coz all she sees is his stupid face."

"Why do you have to hide then?" Anna's voice is softer now. She remembers the rage in her own mum's voice, yelling about Anna's awful destiny to be just like Andy McVay.

"It's for safety. She's really annoyed with dad, so she sent some bad guys after us. He said she'll take me away to get back at him," Alice shrugs. Anna tried not to flinch at the story of their father's blatant self-centered narcissism.

"Have they come before then? The bad guys?"

"Yeah, but they didn't beat up dad before. Usually, we run away before that."

Anna's mind is racing. She has a million questions. She thought she'd had it bad over the years, living in her dad's crooked shadow, but she'd had it easy. Presuming he was dead was a gift compared to what this girl was growing up with.

"So they are after you? Someone might try and take you away?"

"Hmm, the other ones will."

"Wait. Who?" Anna rubbed her face, desperate to get all the information, but so aware that it's just a little child she's asking.

"The men with the same voice as me, they work for my mum. The ones last night had a voice like Christine."

"English accents?"

"Yeah. The ones that got dad last night sounded like, 'I'll fucking kull hum,'" she put on a broad Scottish accent, and Anna laughed. "The normal bad guys sound like "Alright sweetheart, how's it going?" This time her accent was exaggerated cockney. They both laughed at her impressions for a second before a wave of panic hit Anna.

She picked Alice up, onto her back and looked around them. Things just got a lot more complicated. If the Docherty's weren't their only concern, then tonights digging operation would need more planning.

At least she could recognise a gypsie coming. She had no idea who else she was looking for.

"Do you think you'd recognise them? The English guys?"

"Well, maybe. I have seen them but i might of forgot what they look like."

Anna quickened her pace, the unease rising up her spine, as it dawned on her that she shouldn't be out on the street. And, she definitely should not have taken Alice.

"Put your hood up, please, pull it tight round your face." She was panting now, heading along the route Claire would have always taken to Christine's. In her plan, she would simply bump into her halfway along the path; then they'd all have been safely inside within ten minutes. But there was no sign of her. She couldn't think of anywhere else to look. Claire wouldn't have gone to visit anyone. She wouldn't be roaming the shops. There's no way she'd have nipped into the Nag's Head for a drink. Could she?

Her instincts were pulling her apart inside. She wanted to hide Alice from whatever unknown danger she was in, and she needed to find Claire.

"Can you whistle?" she asked, hoisting Alice's legs up higher on her hips as they bounced along the pavement. From above her head, she heard puffing, blowing, and high-pitched squeals.

"Ok, I'll teach you. Then, if you see anyone bad, any danger at all, that can be our sign."

"I always wanted to learn how to whistle." Her voice sounded thrilled. Anna puzzled at the joy she was finding in this terrible situation.

She dropped Alice on a swing at the park, pulled her hood around her face, and gave her a gentle push while watching the perimeter for Claire.

She tried to make some order of what was going on, she always felt better once things were listed, but it was useless.

Her palms were sweating as her brain fought to make sense of it all. Having this unknown, faceless danger was worse than any Gypsy or plastic gangster she already had to worry about. The image of her dad's bruised face, crusty blood still lining the rim of his nose, and the white of one eye streaked with burst red veins flooded back to her. She was feeling a little faint; the constant head-turning on the lookout was making her dizzy. Claire probably just needed a break from everything. She was probably just getting some quiet time away from the twins and Jean's constant talking.

"Come on, let's get back. It's too cold out here." She held the chains to slow the swing and helped her off.

"What about your friend?"

"She'll be ok. I'm sure she's fine."

Anna

Back at Christine's, they enter to the swooshing sound of bleach being sprayed on the kitchen worktop.

"You're in so much trouble. Andy's furious you took her out again."

Anna felt anger rise in her chest.

"Are you kidding me? He's not been my Dad in a decade, but now I'm in trouble?"

"The bairns no supposed to go out."

"Aye, and did he tell you why? Because there's all sorts of folk after them. No just the Dougherty's, some English guys are hunting them too. Have been for a long time by the sounds of it."

Christine scrubbed harder, not looking up.

"You already know this, don't you?" Anna

moved to try and catch her eye. "What's he told you? I've got a right to know if we are in danger."

Christine sprayed more bleach, refolded her cloth, and scrubbed some more.

Anna gave up and went into the living room, steeling herself to ask him some tough questions, but she was frozen to the spot by the scene before her.

Alice was sitting on his knee, with her head resting on his chest, as he gently stroked her hair from her forehead. He smiled and beckoned Anna over. Reluctantly she sat on the edge of the sofa, unable to be part of the sweet family scene.

"I know you've been looking after Alice, but I'd really appreciate it if you didn't take her out of the house." He said softly, still stroking her head.

Anna sat up a little straighter and dug her nails into her palms.

"And why's that then?"

"After last night, I don't want her out there in the firing line of the Dougherty's, god knows what they are capable of."

"Right. Obviously. The Dougherty's. No one else we should worry about?"

Alice made a face that said, 'please don't

get me in trouble'. Andy wriggled in his seat a little. He cleared his throat, "ok, I should explain. Things have been, you know, a bit..."

"Complicated? I should have guessed. You know that excuse is played out? That word doesn't mean anything. Can you just tell me the truth?"

He sighed, and a cough followed. He covered his swollen mouth with a bruised hand. His entire body shook as he coughed until it finally slowed down. He looked tired, defeated; he nodded.

"We need to get what we came here for, tonight. Before anyone else does. Some old mates of mine, we had a bit of a fallout see. They said they were going to take the money. It was a misunderstanding though, not my fault, but they won't listen, so we need to get it first...."

Anna's eyes had glazed over as she drifted in and out. She could hear him, as if she was inside a glass bowl; his words were fuzzy at the other side. While inside, her own voice was clear as day, telling her this was all bullshit. They weren't old friends, and there was no misunderstanding. The truth was a whole different thing, and he had no intention of telling her. So she nodded, accepting, with no further questioning. It would be pointless. Just like her Mum used to tell her.

"Well, we better get prepared for digging then," she interrupted his trailing lies and pushed forward with the plan. "So, can you whistle? Because we need an alarm call."

Andy looked taken aback that she wasn't interested in what he was saying.

"I can whistle now! Listen!" Alice tried a few times, failing and lisping, then she produced a perfect, loud, high-pitched tone and looked surprised at herself. "Anna taught me!"

"You can look out from upstairs." Anna said, "Whistle if you see anything, police, gypsies. Anyone else." She said the last words extra slowly, keeping his eye in hers, but he looked away.

"Good plan." He said, "Alice, I think you should just stay safe in the cupboard till we are all done, ok?"

"I'll whistle if anyone comes in the cupboard then."

Anna smiled at her enthusiasm and said, "I'm going to get some old clothes to wear, I've got the spade sorted, and we've got the map ready. Now we just need to wait till the right time."

Anna left them practicing whistling and went to find Christine. She stood in the doorway watching her wring out a steaming cloth. The water was so hot her hands were the colour of boiled crabs. She wiped down the cupboard doors and went for more scalding water. She jumped when she noticed Anna watching.

"You ok? Get everything sorted?" she asked.

"He's hiding something. Probably a lot of things actually. I'll never know the truth. So for now, tonight, I'm going to see if he has any honesty in him at all. Or, if all this buried money nonsense is just another pile of shit."

"Do you not think it's real?" Christine checked over her shoulder and wrinkled her nose up.

"God knows. But if it is, I'm taking my share, and I'm out of here. That pair can go and get on with their life, wherever it is they came from."

Christine narrowed her eyes," That's it? You'll just go your separate ways?"

"Aye, I don't need them. It's just trouble I can do without."

CHAPTER FIFTEEN

15

Anna

Anna watches the golden pendulum swing below the black glass clock. She listens to the ticking as she watches Christine and Gina get into a taxi on the street below. Christine was awkwardly holding the door open for Gina in the rain. She looks up to the window above and gives the nod to Andy watching from the bedroom.

Anna's legs swoosh as she walks in the old shell suit trousers she found, knowing she looks ridiculous, but they will only be fit for the bin once she's dragged herself through the mud looking for the mythical tubes full of cash.

As she swishes into the cupboard under the stairs to get the spade, she whispers into the darkness, "You ok in there?"

"Yes, I am. Are you going to be ok going out there?" Alice replied.

"Of course, I'll be fine." She felt a slight twinge of something, gratitude perhaps, that someone so little, who didn't even know her would genuinely be concerned if she was ok.

The drizzle tickles her face as she stands on the doorstep. Everything seems a lot harder now she's there, in the cold, wet reality. The fence is higher than she imagined, the garden seems more exposed than she'd pictured, and it was far darker than anticipated. She wanted to chuck the spade down, go get Claire, and hop on a train home to Edinburgh. Claire! How could she have forgotten to call Jean's again? She should have checked she was ok. What an awful friend. A greasy guilty feeling twisted in her belly. She'd be fine. Wouldn't she? She'd of heard otherwise. Someone would have been round to Christine's looking if she wasn't. Yeah, it's fine, she told herself, whispering into the rain, "let's get this over with and get on with our bloody lives."

The wind was picking up, whistling through the bare branches and smashing a wind-chime off a distant washing line. She swung her leg over the fence, slipping a little in the flower border. She thought back to the map drawn with felt tips, the charming daisies and the cute frogs, how innocent it all looked, when the reality was - dirty money in frozen mud, with who knows what consequences to come.

Shoving the spade in the first corner was easy. The ground was so wet it reminded her of the texture of mud-pies. The same mud-pies she'd made in that very garden all those years ago, while listening to her mum talking to Christine. Maybe laughing, maybe crying, but her dad was always at the center of it. All emotions revolved around him. His presence, his absence, his lies, and sometimes even harsher truths. Now here she was, digging for something that might not exist, while he watches out of the window.

She started to laugh, then tears joined in, as she imagined her mum shaking her head at the madness of this situation.

Then the spade felt different. It bounced

off something. She tested the earth around it, scraped some mud back, revealing a glimmer of white, shining amber in the streetlight. She got on her knees and wiped the earth back till she found the end.

Was it true?

A sealed white tube, buried 12 inches below the surface. She'd found one. When she freed it from the earth's grip, she shook it, feeling heavy contents sliding inside.

Fucking hell, he's actually telling the truth!

Spurred on, she slammed the spade into the next area, hoping for that same smooth thud of the spade on the white plastic treasure. The hole was getting wider. Her foot slid in. She starts refiling it, knocking the pile into the hole and moving her target area over a bit. She's getting tired, and begins to think he's exaggerated. Maybe there is only one?

Then the spade bounces back, the vibration up the handle tells her she's found what she's looking for. Back on her knees, she uses her hands to reveal the light plastic, then pulls it out with a slop and a pop.

With the two tubes side by side resting against the fence, she takes aim again, in the opposite corner near the gate, till she's stopped by a whistle. She hesitates, listening hard to differentiate between the wind and a warning. Then it comes again, three short blasts. She crouches down, watching the road as lights approach, holding her breath, hoping for it to pass, it's slow, but it doesn't stop.

She begins to feel very vulnerable; if someone did come now, they could take what she'd found; it was laid out on the ground for whoever wanted to take the chance.

More car light crest the hill, coming her way.

Water was seeping into her gloves, her teeth chattered. She'd take these in, store them safely, get warmed up, then come back out. Maybe the rain and wind would ease off a bit and make it easier.

Her shoes were caked in solid mud, she couldn't wipe it off, and she couldn't bear Christine's wrath if she dragged this much mud in, so she kicked them off at the step.

She ran the hot tap; clear water turned brown as she watched the mud run from her fingers. As the heat crept back into her fingers, they burned, then ached.

Anna

Drips of brown muddy water circle Anna's feet; she wipes them away with a tea towel, then dries her hands. She hears Andy's feet on the stairs and feels his presence behind her. She can't turn round. She keeps drying her hands, rubbing the towel between her fingers.

"Will you manage to get the rest?" He asks, leaning on the worktop beside her and shaking a tube next to his ear, "We need to do this tonight."

"Why tonight? What's the hurry? They've been neglected in under there for ten years. Another day or so won't make much difference."

"We don't have much time Anna, I don't have much time." He coughs. This time she sees a little blood on his cotton hankie.

The words bounce off her. Part of her heard, the same part that saw the blood, but the rest of her chose to ignore it.

"Tonight, tomorrow, next week, it's all the same. And, it would be better doing it when it's not raining."

"Anna, my darling. I might not be here

then, and I need to see you two girls have the money and are safe."

"You've only just got here. Surely you can hang around for a while." Her voice is trembling. She looks away as he limps closer.

"I'm dying Anna, at best, I've got a month."

She shook her head and pulled away.

"I only just found out. I thought it was a chest infection, had a cough for as long as I can remember, all those Benson and Hedges, I guess."

"Don't be stupid. How can you be dying? I've not seen you for years. You can't just show up on your death bed,"

"He is Anna," Alice said from the door, "the hospital man told us last week, so we came to find you straight away."

Andy took Anna by the shoulders. He looked older and weaker by the minute.

"I need to know you'll be ok." He said.

She shrugged free of his grip,

"Of course I'll be ok. I've been ok this far without you. I'll just go back..."

She tried to turn away, but he took her shoulders again, "I need to know you'll look after Alice."

Anna looked in stunned silence through full eyes, from her Dad's face to the sad-looking young girl in the doorway.

"I'm all she's got, and you're sisters, blood-related. She needs you." Andy pleaded.

Anna's mouth opens, but she doesn't know what's going to come out...

Then, Bang! The front door swings open. There's a struggle in the hall.

"McVay! Get out here now!"

Anna recognised that voice,

"Fuuuck!" She drags Alice into the living room and pulls the sofa from the wall. "Get behind there!" Alice squeezes on all fours into the darkness just as the door's kicked open.

Ronin fills the doorway, dragging Claire by the neck in the crook of his arm. Anna sees the terror in her eyes, a dirty rag tied round her mouth, blood-stained and wet, with hair sticking to her face, she runs towards Claire, but she's held back by the gun Ronin's waving between them.

"Where's your father?" He shouts.

Anna looks around for him, but he's gone. He's left her to deal with this herself—the absolute bastard.

"He's in the hospital, you should know.

Your brothers put him in there," Anna shouts back, trying to get closer to Claire.

He's holding her round the neck with his arm, dragging her, digging a wooden-handled pistol into her chin, then directing it at Anna.

"Don't you lie to me again. You owe me a lot of money! I'm taking it back now, or I'm taking it out on your friend here." He jabbed the gun into her chin harder; Claire made what little noise she could with her mouth gagged.

"Let her go. I've got money. You can have all of it, just let her go."

"Show me the fucking money, right now, or I'll blow her fucking jaw off."

Anna put her hands up, trying to calm him, "Ok, it's in here, there's a lot, I'll get it, just let her go. Please!"

"I fell for your bullshit once. I won't do it again. You give me the money, or I'll shoot her right now, and you'll be picking your wee pal's brains out of your hair for weeks. Money! Now!"

"It's through here," she walked backward with her hands up, he dragged Claire into the kitchen.

Anna passed him the two mud-stained

cylinders, "Take them, I don't know how much is in there, but it's more than I owe you."

"You think I'm a mug? I'm not taking a couple of tubes away on your word!" They're probably empty. Open them first. Let me see." He pulls Claire's neck; her eyes are streaming.

"Ok, ok, I need something to cut it with." Anna pulled open the drawers, found a bread knife, and began carving. Little curls of white plastic fell to the floor; her hand ached, she sawed and sawed but made little progress. She pushed harder as she heard Claire whimper from inside his grasp.

"Try something else!" He shouted. Anna looked at Claire's pleading eyes, then raised the tube above her head and slammed it onto the edge of the dirty counter. It cracked, she pulled it apart and gasped as rolls of £100 notes as thick as coke cans thumped onto the ground. He pushed Claire out of the way, and used one hand to throw the rolls into his pockets, while still waving the gun between them. Claire was slumping down the side of the fridge to the ground in pain and shock. Anna stood in front of her, blocking Ronin's reach.

He picked up the second tube and felt its weight. He backed out of the door laughing, "That's us even now, McVay. Tell your father I'm coming for him next." He turned and jumped down all the steps at once and leapt over the gate.

Anna unties the gag from Claire's mouth and wipes the hair from her face,

"I'm so sorry, I'm so sorry, I knew something wasn't right, I looked for you, but I couldn't find you. Oh my god, what happened?"

Claire rubbed her mouth. Her eyes were bloodshot, and tears streamed, "Where the fuck did all the money come from?"

Ronin

We've hit the big time! Hillary, there's thousands and thousands of pounds in here!" He threw the gun onto the seat, then the tube onto her lap, followed by rolls of £100 notes.

"Oh my goodness," Hillary smiled, with her whole body, a joy he'd never seen before. She filled her old green Gucci shopping bag, stroking each bundle in turn.

"And you think the same is in this one?" she shook the tube.

"Even more by the weight of it. Come on, Hillary, this is it. Let's get out here. For good."

"Oh, but what about your family? Don't you want to avenge your grandfather?"

"My family?" Ronin started pulling his earlobe as he drove, "You don't even like my family, I thought you wanted to leave?"

"But don't you want to get Andy McVay and hand him over? I thought you wanted to be the one everyone thanked? Unless you don't mind your brothers thinking you're scared."

"I'm not scared, woman! But this is our chance; we've enough money there to never come back."

"Ok, let's leave it. Leave Andy McVay to get away and forget how he disrespected your grandfather. It wont matter what your Dad thinks of you once we are away." Hillary pulled the gold zip closed and patted the heavy bag on her knee.

Ronin was bouncing on the seat, he could almost feel the steam coming out of his ears.

"No, he's gone, leave them to it. My family can deal with him when they find him."

"But you could just get him from the hospital and deliver him straight to your father."

"He's not at the hospital. Tina and Maria tried there, forget him, let's just go."

"The least we can do is check, come along. I'll quickly go in and find out his whereabouts."

"Then what?"

"I'll convince him to take a walk with me, and then you grab him into the back of the van. Like you did earlier. Wouldn't it be worth it to see the look on your brother's faces when you deliver what none of them could? Don't you deserve this?"

Ronin blew out from puffed-out cheeks, "Aye, I deserve it alright. I'll be the one to finish the job. I'll bring him in."

"Good, now go left here. We'll go the back way."

"This isn't the way to the hospital, woman. This takes us out towards the bridge," he slowed at the junction, hesitating.

"We need to go the back way. Those girls have probably called the police."

"Fuck!" He slammed the steering wheel and growled with his teeth bared.

"Did you think you could take a young woman hostage and no one would have anything to say about it?" Hillary's almost laughing.

"They won't phone the polis. That lot are as crooked as they come," he swung the van into the junction.

"Take the next right," Hillary said, pointing out a narrow side road between a row of gardens.

He braked hard; they slid forward in their seats, "Are you sure that leads to the hospital?"

"I know all the back roads. I used to ride them all on my horse, remember?"

He didn't reply, there was too much guilt hanging on any conversation about her horse. The lane narrowed as they proceeded, branches scraped the sides, the wheels bumped down in the hollows of puddles. Then, they came face to face with another car. It was in darkness, empty, blocking the path.

"That's my old escort! Those English bastards must have dumped it here. Fuck sake, I'll have to reverse all the way back." He put the van into gear, and opened the window, leaned his head out to see the path behind. Then he felt cold metal on his chin, tilting his head up.

"Put your hands where I can see um. Both of them." Ronin recognised the voice and raised his hands. The headlights opposite lit up their faces. Frankie reached in, turned the van off, and took the keys.

"Get the gun Ronin," Hillary whispered from his side, "point it at him, get the keys back."

Her door opened, and Billy wrapped his huge hand around her throat.

"Give me the money, all of it, right now!" He growled close to her face.

"We don't have any money! Anna has it, back at that house, they've got thousands, we couldn't..."

Ronin glanced automatically at the bag on her knee, then straight ahead, hoping no one noticed in the dark.

"Ah, ha," Billy laughed as he lifted the handle. He unzipped it, looked inside and nodded to Frankie.

He pulled Hillary by the arm. She struggled, trying to slide away from his grip, "Do something Ronin!" she screamed, as he dragged her out, her protest dulled by the hand over her mouth as he dragged her backward out of the van.

"You don't come after us, you don't phone the pigs, if you do, your missus gets it." He put the keys in his pocket and pushed Ronin's temple with the end of the gun. He walked backward, keeping aim, back behind the lights and into the car. They reversed away, leaving Ronin sitting in the dark.

Hillary

"Now what? There's only one tube and some cash in ere. What about the rest?" Frankie said from the back seat as they reversed onto the main road.

Billy looked in the rearview mirror and replied, "We go down there and finish this job. Force him to hand over the rest, and then we finish whoever's in there, McVay, the kid, and whoever else. I'm done with this place."

Hillary dabbed her eyes with a hankie, applied a fresh layer of lipstick, then added,

"Apparently, they are adamant he's still in hospital, and he didn't show face when the girls were under threat, so perhaps we should check."

"We saw him up at the window back there

this morning."

"Did you actually see him though? I never, I just took your word for it."

"Yeah, I mean, I'm fairly sure. But he definitely wasn't in the hospital this morning. We checked."

"Perhaps he told the nurse to tell you that? If I were on the run from you two, I certainly wouldn't be allowing random visitors to my bedside." Hillary said, checking her lips in the passenger mirror.

"She's got a point. Maybe we should try again. We can't let him get away this time."

"I don't know. It's a bit jail bait, the pigs could be hanging around the hospital."

"I'm sure you boys know what you're doing, but here's an idea. Why don't you go into the hospital," she taps Billy's knee, and gives it a little squeeze. "You find him and let him know we have his girls, and he needs to hand over the money. If he's not there, well, we still have the girls, and that's the kind of leverage we need. They'll know how to contact him, and he'll come to us if he knows we have a gun and his daughters."

"That's what I was thinking," Billy said as he did a u-turn and headed back towards the hospital.

"I'm not going in there again. I fucking hate hospitals." Frankie said as they slowed at the brightly lit entrance. "I'll keep the gun, and you get in there. You only need to find him and tell him we've got the girls."

"Fuck sake," Billy grunted as he got out into the rain.

Frankie got into the driver's seat and wiped the mist from the side window.

"Full of good ideas you are," he said, smiling. Hillary placed her hand on his thigh,

"I need out of this god-forsaken town, and I'll do whatever it takes to do it," she trailed her fingers lightly up and down, from knee to groin.

"You certainly will," he laughed, "you proved that earlier."

"Mm-mm, that was nice," she purred, trailing her finger further up each time. She watched his breathing change. Satisfied he was occupied in his memory, she slid the black handgun from his lap and sat back, shining it up on her sleeve.

"Oi, careful with that. It's loaded."

"It's ok, I know what I'm doing," she clicked it open and closed, marveling at the smoothness compared to Ronin's antique.

She felt its weight in each hand and practiced holding it, closing one eye to aim out ahead.

"Alright, that's plenty. You're making me nervous. Put in down."

She obliged, sliding it carefully between his legs, then brushing her fingers back down his thigh. "So, how much more do you reckon there is?"

"Twice that at least, good few grand in it for you, since you've been such a help."

"Indeed." Hillary smiled as they entered Green Street.

CHAPTER SIXTEEN

16

Anna

After the noise of Ronin's van had faded away, Anna secured the house and got a warm blanket.

Claire sat staring straight ahead, her eyes like glass, her face scratched and blotchy. Anna took her hand and asked, "what happened?"

Claire's mouth quivers, she looks at the ground, starts to talk but her voice breaks; she tries to clear her throat, but stops, interrupted by a shadow in the doorway.

Anna follows her gaze to see Andy, slow and sheepish, edging his way into the living room.

"Where the fuck did you go?" she stands up, arms waving in frustration, "You left me there to deal with them. He had a fucking gun! What kind of father are you?" Anna shouted; she wanted to hit him so badly. She held back, suddenly aware of the big brown eyes watching from below.

"I gave him that money, every fucking penny. Look what they did to Claire because of you."

"That's ok. We can get the rest. There's much more than that still buried."

"Seriously? Look at the problems this has caused! You dig it up, I'm taking Claire, and we are leaving. Do you see what they did to her, because of you! I wish I'd never come back here."

"No, Anna, wait, we need you, Alice needs you."

"I'm out of here. You want that money? You find it. You want someone to look after your golden child? You find someone else!"

Alice pulls her hand. Anna avoids looking; Alice pulls harder, "Please, dad can't dig, and I'm too small. Just help me one more time, then you can go home."

Anna saw Claire looking between Anna

and Alice. The freckles, the shape of the nose, the colour of their hair.

"Oh yeah, did no one mention I have a sister now?" Anna said, anger overflowing, as Claire went to Alice's side and offered out a hand.

"Pleased to meet you. I'm Claire."

"Please," Andy said, "We've got almost an hour left. Gina will be back soon. I need you to have this money before I'm gone. If it's not for me, or your little sister, do it for yourself. It's your inheritance."

Anna watched the realisation on Claire's face, "Oh yeah, and my dad's going to be dead soon! There's been a lot going on since you were abducted because of him!"

"Right, Anna, come on." Claire used the tone that always grounded her, "Has anyone got a plan then?"

"What? Let's just get out of here!" Anna said, shocked at Claire's response.

"We've come this bloody far, and you've no idea the day I've had. If there's anything to be gained from this shit show, let's get it."

Anna

"Dad, you look out from the upstairs window, keep it open, and whistle if you see anyone coming. Claire, you take Alice into the cupboard and wait there till I come and get you, ok?"

"I'm not hiding in the cupboard," Claire looked confused.

"I always hide in the cupboard, it's fine when you get used to it. It starts off black, and you can't see anything, but soon you can see a little bit. Come on, I'll show you." Alice pulled her towards the stairs and Anna gave Claire a secret look that said 'wait till I tell you the rest,' as she disappeared inside.

Anna's hands were horribly dry, she felt the mud crack and flake from her knuckles.

"Will you make it upstairs?" she asked, as Andy steadied himself with both hands on the breakfast bar.

He nodded and tilted his head to invite her closer. She looked away. "Come on," he put his arm out. She avoided his eyes but awkwardly moved into the space he'd made for her.

He hugged her close, with one arm still holding him steady. She felt him tremble and heard his shallow breath in her ear. She noticed now how thin he was under his clothes. She remembered hugging him all those years ago, feeling safe in his massive arms, now he felt like a fragile old man.

"Isn't there anything the doctors can do for you?" she whispered.

"A couple of years ago maybe, but it's too late now. My time's up. I'm so glad I managed to see you first, to say goodbye. And to say sorry."

Anna felt her face getting red, her eyes filling with tears. She buried her face in his shoulder so he couldn't see her while she silently let them flow.

"I know I haven't been the best Dad, to either of you, and I'm sorry. There's so much I should of done differently."

She felt him check his watch over her shoulder, she pulled away, caught the worst of the tears on her sleeves, and said,

"You know I've never been abroad? When I was little, you said you'd take me to Disney land. I believed you for a long time."

"I meant to; things just got..."

"Complicated. I know. You keep saying," Anna laughed and broke the painful mood. He smiled back, his eyes sparkling like she remembered.

"There's enough money there for a hundred trips to Disney land, if that's what you want?"

"I'm a bit old for that, but we could go somewhere, we'll have time. Won't we?"

"The three of us? My two beautiful daughters and their old dad. I'd like that."

Anna dried the last of her tears, streaking brown mud down her face. "Well, I better get digging then, eh? Before we run out of time completely."

Claire

Inside the cupboard, Claire talks gently to Alice. She's used to getting information from her nephews without causing a fuss.

"Was it a surprise to meet your big sister?"

"No, I already knew. I wanted to meet her since I was a baby probably."

Claire wouldn't normally sit in darkness this black. She'd leave doors open, keep a hall light on, or leave a gap in the curtains to let some street light in. This kind of darkness was thick; she could feel it on her skin.

"Do you ever get bored sitting on your own?" Claire asked.

"Yeah, sometimes Dad's away for ages, but he always brings back something good. Like a magazine, or a sweet or something."

"That's nice, I suppose. Do you get scared?"

"Not really. Dad says I'll always be safe if I hide, so I don't need to be scared."

"True. So, what is it you're hiding from?"

"Probably my Mum. And some bad guys coz of complicated things about money. Usually that."

"Does your Mum want you to come home? But your Dad wants you to stay with him?"

"No, she doesn't like me. She says I'm a horrible brat. And, she hates Dad too, so we have to hide."

Claire feels tears building up, suddenly grateful for the darkness.

"She probably doesn't hate you, you know. She might just have a lot of problems, so she acts like she does. She might actually be really sad."

"I don't think so. She says I can just get adopted, because I'm too bad to stay with her."

"Are you bad?"

"I don't know, I just always want to see

my dad and not her, coz she's horrible."

"She might not mean these things. My mum was pretty horrible to me when I was little, but she didn't mean it. She was just messed up about other stuff. Maybe she does care."

"No, she really doesn't, but I don't mind because now I've found my sister, and she's going to look after me when Dad dies."

Once again Claire's glad they can't see each other's faces. Her pained expression would definitely upset Alice.

"That's nice," she gulps down the sorrow and clears her throat, "you're lucky you've found her. Anna will be a great big sister."

"I know, Dad told me."

Claire can't talk. She's no idea what to say to this helpless child whose broken world is about to be turned upside down.

Anna

Anna walked behind Andy on the stairs, willing him to hurry up, while praying he didn't tumble backward. He coughed and stopped to catch his breath every few steps. She opened the blinds and pulled Christine's chair to the window. From the darkness of the room he could see up the hill, into the park and most of the path towards the houses.

The wind was picking up, the last of the Autumn leaves were swirling around like black bats. The rain was getting heavier. The road surface shimmered as the water ran down the hill like a river.

Anna opened the window a couple of inches, the rain roared, and the wind thrashed bare branches.

"The garden's different to what I remember, but it's there. Two feet from the wall, two feet from the path. Right there, he pointed to Alice's map. The spot right underneath a cartoon frog. "The other is at the foot of the tree, facing away from the house."

"It's fine. I'll measure from each side and dig through the lawn. It's too dark for Gina to notice when she gets in. She'll just think it's a molehill in the morning."

Giant raindrops reflected the street lights as they rolled diagonally across the glass, blown sideways by the wind.

"Wish me luck," she said while zipping Christine's old purple anorak up to her chin.

"Be as quick as you can, but be careful."

"Just whistle, and I'll get out of there," she left the room but stuck her head back in when he called,

"Anna," his voice was hoarse, "I, I love you. Very much."

She nodded at his dark silhouette against the stormy window, then took a deep breath and jumped down the stairs two at a time.

She measured the distance from the wall and the fence, looking up and down the windy road before plunging the spade into the ground. She lifted heavy wet mud and tipped it into the corner. The wind whipped her hair into her eyes, and rain dripped off her nose.

A big cold drip rolled down her neck, all the way to her cosy soft belly. Her hands were numb, the kind of numb that you know will be burning agony when you get inside, like the aftermath of sledging with no gloves on.

The hole was getting silly now, it was huge, and there was no sign of any tubes. The wind blew the gate open, she jumped, her legs went to jelly, and she felt sick. She didn't know how long was left, but she knew it wasn't long. She pushed wet strands of hair behind her ears and forced herself to dig faster.

Then it hit, the spade slid to the side, she felt the smooth curve of resistance in the earth. She got on her knees and thrust her hands into the freezing hole, and frantically pushed earth from the length of it, feeling around for the end. With the edge exposed, she used the spade as a lever till it popped from one side. She pulled it out and pushed it up inside her jacket. She pulled the drawstrings at the bottom to hold it in. She was past caring about mud and the cold.

She dug desperately till she felt that familiar smoothness of a tube. She used her hands to uncover its shape. It was thinner this time, a different kind to the others. With the spade wedged underneath, she pushed and forced with her weight. It wouldn't give as easy as the last. Maybe it was longer. She kicked the spade deeper underneath and raised her foot onto the handle, and jumped. It finally gave, followed by a hiss, then a rush of water. The hole was filling up, the top rippled with heavy raindrops still falling.

She truly wanted to give up, call it a night and crawl into a dry bed, forget any of this was happening. But she knew, if she'd burst the water pipe, they'd need to dig it up to fix it. Then someone else would find the other tubes. There was no way; she couldn't risk that.

She grit her teeth, spat "fuck sake," from between them, and started digging again. Faster than before, throwing wet mud anywhere now. The shell suit trousers were soaked and sticking to her thighs, mud and freezing water squelched between her toes inside her shoes. Drips rolled down her face and neck into her jacket.

Finally, she hit a tube. Back on her knees, she plunged her hand into the area she'd felt the spade bounce. The water was past her elbows, it seeped up her sleeves as she scrambled around in the mud. She pulled, leaned back, and pulled again. It came free with a force that threw her back onto the ground, covering with a wave of mud as she fell backward.

She slid to her feet, looking at the overflowing hole and devastated corner of her old childhood garden.

One more to go, under the tree. She pushed the tube up inside her coat to join the other, and prepared to find the exact point of the final one.

She looked up at the dark window her Dad was watching from, inside the house where her best friend and Alice were safe in the cupboard.

An uneasy feeling made her forget she was cold and wet, when she saw the living room blinds. They were uneven. There was a bowed one in the middle, creating an untidy gap. This was new.

She shakes it off, knowing there's possibly only minutes left to get the last one before the chance is gone. She drops the sharp edge on the spade into the ground and looks back up at the window. It's not right. Something's not right. She leaves the spade, jumps over the fence, and opens the front door.

Andy

Andy remembers the exact day he buried them there. Anna and her mum had arrived back from shopping in town, and he was reading the paper in the garden. Debbie asked why the earth was disturbed; he'd said something ridiculous about growing his own food. By that point she hadn't believed a thing he'd said for a while. She'd just given him that look, and ushered Anna in with the bags.

He'd only planned on staying away a couple of months. He'd thought he'd be back there, digging it up and doing his usual - begging for forgiveness and promising he'd be a better husband.

He really was going to, but once he met Angelica, and got involved in her business, cold boring Scotland didn't seem so appealing. His new lifestyle suited him better - the clothes, the cars, the restaurants, the coke.

Pangs of guilt would surface daily, to begin with, then less and less as his old life faded into the background. When he did think about them, he'd promise himself, at the end of the month, once that jobs done, once the next deal comes off, when things settled down a bit, when he got a break, soon, he'd go back home and make a mends.

The buried money had been a safety net, he'd never been short after that, so keeping it in the background was just a little security. No point wasting it then, when things were good. He knew in the back of his mind the highs couldn't last forever, and one day he'd need to come back and find it, but not then. Not when him and Angelica were so happy, not once the baby came, and not when everything changed.

He thought back to the last time he'd seen Angelica, the hate in her eyes for him, and the indifference for her own child. He always wondered how the two women of his life story had been so different. Debbie and Angelica, two more opposite women you couldn't imagine. One soft, maternal and kind, the other hard, driven and cruel.

He'd driven them both mad, of course, with his terrible excuses and selfish behavior.

He never knew in advance if something was selfish or not. Only when someone was screaming it in his face. He couldn't predict either of their reaction and gave up trying. He'd collected a list of things he'd done that were 'selfish,' so sometimes tried to avoid repeating them, but he usually forgot or managed to justify his actions. Things he thought were fine and reasonable often turned out to be 'thoughtless' and 'self-centered.' It was only becoming clear to him now, as he approached the end, where exactly the center ought to be.

The rain was lashing the windows, and the wind was picking up again. In the distance, he heard thunder rumble, or a bucket tumble. He stood and peered down at the top of Anna's head, the streetlight making her glow orange as she dug up her future, and his past.

He wobbled back down onto the chair, relieved to take the weight off after just a few seconds. He smiled as he pictured her, just like her mum, never scared to get her hands dirty. He didn't think Angelica had ever even touched the earth.

A little draft pushed the bedroom door open with a creak. He pulled himself back up on the side of the dressing table; Anna was still out there, the street was empty.

CHAPTER SEVENTEEN

17

Claire

Claire had to know what was happening out there, or at least how much time they had left. She opened the little angled door slightly, the soft grey light is a relief from the solid black of the cupboard.

"We should wait. My Dad will..." Alice is cut off by Claire,

"Shh, did you hear that?"

"Shut the door, be quiet."

"It's ok, someones out the back, hold on, I'll check." Claire crept out and slowly moved through the hall into the kitchen. The back door curtain was open, and through the mottled glass, she saw a figure.

"It's just Anna," Claire reassures Alice.

"It might not be her, you should come back in here,"

"Course it's her. Who else would try the door? Someone must have come to the front. I'm letting her in."

The seed of doubt planted by Alice grew as she approached the door. The figure was lit from the back. It was distorted and dark; she could see thin legs, a narrow frame, definitely female. The figure tapped gently on the glass with fingertips as Claire approached. She sighed relief and turned the key, ready to get Anna in and lock it behind her.

"No!" Claire tries to push the door closed on Hillary. "You can't come in here, get away," With just a few inches left to close, a larger, man's figure shoves Hillary out of the way and puts his foot inside the door. Claire pushes it with all her weight, but it's no match for him. She slides backward on the lino and gets trapped between the door and fridge.

"Get out..." Claire shouts, her voice cracking with pain as her sore wrists buckle under the strain of holding his weight behind the door. He releases the pressure, she slips and scrambles to get away, she trips through the living room, stumbling over the footstool by the window, she feels him grab the back of her top and haul her to her feet, a terrified squeal escapes as she tries to wriggle free. He forces her up and pushes her against the blinds.

He puts a massive hand over her mouth and whispers, "Keep it down, sweetheart, unless you want a bullet through your head."

Claire feels the cold metal on her temple, she nods.

"Now, tell me where Andy McVay is."

Claire's silent. She knows he's upstairs, she holds her eyes on the man's face, hoping she doesn't give it away by looking up. She hears the steps on the stairs, and then his telltale cough. She won't let herself look anywhere. She closes her eyes, the gun still pressed against her temple and her blood rushing through her legs, her instincts telling her to curl up and hide. His huge hands drop Claire when he catches a glimpse of Andy on the stairs. He's holding one hand up in surrender, and the other steadying himself on the banister.

"Let the girl go, it's nothing to do with

her." He wheezes at the foot of the stairs, now holding both hands up in the dimly lit hallway.

"I don't think so Andy. Tell you what, I'll do a little swap. You give me the money. I'll give you the girl."

"I don't have it. The gypsy and his Mrs took it," he said as he entered the living room with his hands up. When he saw Hillary, his expression changed.

"Don't you worry, mate," Frankie smiled, "I've got that, now I'm here for the rest."

"There is no more. The rest was spent years ago."

Frankie shook his head and pushed Claire hard against the window, cracking the blinds as he prodded her with the gun.

"The rest, I said. You know what I'm talking about. Where is she?" His teeth clenched, each word ripped through his lips with a poisonous edge.

"She's not here. She's away. She's being looked after somewhere, safe from you and Angelica."

"She wants her back, and everything else that belongs to her."

"Please, let the lassie go. She's nothing to do with any of this." He gestured towards

Claire.

Anna

From behind him, the front door swung open. Anna stood, covered in mud, jaw dropped at the scene before her.

Hillary stepped forward, placing a hand on Frankie's shoulder as his grip tightened on Claire once more.

"I think it would be best for everyone if the money was handed over immediately, before anyone else got hurt."

"Here," Anna began pulling at the soaking cord from around her waist, "Let her go, and I'll give you these."

"No," Andy put his weak arm up as a barrier.

"Yes," Anna said, "this money has brought nothing but trouble. They can fucking have it."

"I knew it," Frankie pointed the gun at Anna while she struggled with the muddy zip and her cold fingers. "Hurry up," he shouted, holding the gun inches from her.

Andy slumped against the wall, cradling his forehead in his hand. Claire watched Anna through streaming eyes. Hillary placed one hand on her hip, watching as Anna finally produced the two white plastic tubes.

"Here, now get the fuck out and leave us alone!" Anna screamed, shoving the tubes into Frankie's chest.

"Keep it down, you stupid bitch" he backhanded Anna's face, and the tubes fell to the ground. The bile boiled inside her throat, her freezing hands burned, she balled a fist and swung for his face. He batted her hand away before she connected and pushed her backward. She stumbled onto the mantlepiece. The edge dug into her ribs; she was winded. She closed her eyes tight, drawing in breath and strength to go for him again. When she opened them, the barrel of his gun was between her eyes.

Everyones breath was held. Claire shouted at Andy, "Do something!" He stood helpless, shaking.

A small voice came from Anna's side,

"Don't you hurt my sister," Alice grabbed Frankie's coat and kicked the side of his leg. He laughed and placed his hand on her head, pushing her away so she couldn't reach with her feet.

"Here she is, though, the little star of the show. Calm down now, princess."

Andy's face turned to grey.

"Grab her Hillary," Frankie ordered, "take her out to the motor, and tie your scarf round her mouth."

"No," Andy stumbles toward Frankie, "Don't touch her, leave her here."

"No chance, there's too much riding on this," Frankie's gun swings between Andy and Anna.

Anna reaches slowly for Alice's shoulder.

"Get back!" He swings the gun between the three - father and his two daughters.

Anna moves a little closer, willfully ignoring his instructions, "It's the money she wants right?" Anna asks while taking another tiny step closer to Alice's side.

"The money, all the tubes, and this pair out of the picture." He points them out with the gun.

"Perhaps you should just take the money, and let them go," Hillary suggests in a sweet, calming voice.

"I've spent six months on their tail, I'm not doing half a job. Put the tubes in your bag, and take this little brat out to the motor."

Anna glanced up at the black and gold glass clock. It was 9.27, Christine would be back at any second. She dug her nails into her palms and took a deep breath,

"No, you take him, not her. He brought this trouble, she's just a kid." Anna picked Alice up and pointed past his gun, at her Dad. "Take all the tubes, I don't want any of that rotten fucking money, and you take it out on him."

Alice wrapped her arms and legs tight around Anna. Frankie shook his head, "Put her down, she's coming with us," he stepped closer to Anna, pressing the gun in her temple.

Anna held Alice tight, "No, you take the money, and him."

Frankie looked confused, he swung the gun between Andy and Anna, one hand on his head.

Anna looked at her Dad. His face looked young again; his expression said 'thank you,' it was sheer relief. He knew what she was doing.

Frankie let out a frustrated "Fuuuuck!" he pinched the bridge of his nose.

Andy's eyes flicked towards the front

door. Anna took his direction and edged away as he struggled to make his decision.

Anna nodded at her father, her mouth formed a smile, but her eyes said her heart was breaking. In that brief second, she saw the Dad she knew.

Andy stepped forward, with his hand out towards the gun, taking Frankie's full attention.

Anna carried Alice, she pulled Claire with them, and the three of them ran out into the rain.

Anna

Splashing through the freezing water cascading over the road, they heard the gunshot. Alice tried to wriggle down, desperate to run back to her dad. Anna hugged her tighter and ran faster.

Claire slowed, her eyes wide, breathless "Anna, we can't, I can't..." she looked like she was going to faint. Anna swung Alice round, hoisted her up, and put the other arm around Claire's shoulders.

"Come on, we have to move."

A second gunshot rang through the mist.

"Daddy!" Alice cried, Anna sped up.

With Alice on her back, sobbing and clinging round her neck, and Claire limping as fast as she could, they made their way towards the graveyard. The rain was still falling heavy, tears and water washing Anna's face as she gathered them all into the safety of the shadow of the big white angel statue. Crouching there, hidden from sight, shielded from the wind and sheltered from the worst of the rain, Anna stretched her anorak around Alice's shoulders, pulling her trembling body closer.

"I can't believe this, who..." Claire began, "well, who... I just... what the fuck Anna? What's going on?"

Sirens wailed in the distance. Anna shook her head, staring into the darkness.

"Who was that, who just shot your Dad?"

Anna shook her head again, speechless. Through the bare trees, blue lights flashed like a strobe in the misty rain. Alice pulled free from the damp safety of Anna's coat,

"He works for my mum."

CHAPTER EIGHTEEN

18

Billy

Billy was exhausted. He'd used all his niceties to get the information out of the nurse at the hospital. She'd started off with the usual 'patient confidentiality,' but soon enough, she was telling him how weird they all thought it was that he'd just ripped all the tubes off and disappeared.

The walk back through the town to the house was taking too long. Luckily they'd driven this way about four thousand times in the last two days, so he knew where he was going.

He walked fast, angry, freezing and soaking, wondering how the hell Frankie just rolled over and let the stupid posh bitch dish out the orders. She had to go; she was not to be trusted.

His shoe started leaking as he marched along the pavement. He's losing his temper; he vows if Frankie's not up to the job, he's going to take control, get it over with his way, and never come back to this fucking shit hole again. As he reaches the bottom of the hill, the blue lights and buzz of people is a relief.

The job's done.

He heads back to the Ashvale, fantasising about having a bacon buttie in the morning and getting the hell out of Scotland.

He reaches for the door handle, but feels a hand on his shoulder.

"Where's Frankie?" He asks.

Hillary puts her finger to her mouth, "shh, let's get inside," she whispered.

"Sorry darling, this is nothing to do with you," he shrugged his shoulder away from her.

"I think you'll find it is. I've got all the money. He told me to run, to find you, then I heard gunshots. I don't know what happened."

Billy looked past her into the dark street

beyond. Footsteps approached, then faded away as a dog walker passed with a hood pulled down over their face.

"Get in here," he pushed her into the vintage reception; a little bell rang above their head, "Fuck sake," he muttered, while Hillary stood on tiptoes and effortlessly silenced the metallic ringing.

He led the way up the creaking stairs, and along the corridor to room number 7.

She emptied the tubes and rolls of cash onto the bed, his expression changes.

"McVay and the girl, did he do it? Did he finish them?"

"It went wrong. He had a gun, they both had guns. It was all a blur. I had to run, I was so scared, he told me to find you, I didn't know what to do."

Both his hands grasp his skull, he lets out a dull groan.

"Jesus fucking Christ, I got to get out of here. This is a bad joke."

"Take me with you," Hillary said.

"No chance," he shakes his head while emptying one of the tubes onto the bed; he looks inside it. He shakes it and tips it up. He shakes and tips the other two, then holds up the last one. It's still sealed.

"Please? I can't stay here. I helped you get this far. I've nowhere to go." She takes her suede jacket off and hangs it on the back of the chair. Her shirt is see-through where the rain's got in. He can see the pattern of her lace bra.

"Not a hope in hell darling," he laughs as he shakes the tube, looking around the room for something to cut it open.

Hillary reclines on the bed beside the rolls of cash. She unbuttons her blouse, her fingers trail her collar bone, collecting water droplets. He tries not to look as he opens the wardrobe door again.

"Pass it here," she said, standing up and removing her blouse. She stood in jeans and her bra, wet curly tendrils of hair clinging to her neck. She took it from his hands, lifted the foot of the heavy bed frame, and positioned the end of the tube underneath. She turned and sat down quickly on the edge of the mattress.

"That's how you do it," she smiled as white plastic shards pinged across the carpet.

He tipped the rolls onto the bed and peered into the empty tube.

"Aarrggh, fuck sake!" he lay down on his

back and covered his eyes.

Hilary rolled over to face him,

"Are you very close?" she asked in her sweet voice.

"Me and Frankie? Not really, done a few jobs together, this was going to be our last."

"Well, you've got the money, and McVay's gone, so job done."

"Half the job. The kids still out there, and I don't have the fucking envelope." His fists balled, and his jaw tightened.

"You wouldn't really hurt a child, would you?"

"We were supposed to use the kid to make sure we got the rest, but that plans out the window now he's dead."

"What's in the envelope?"

"No idea, but I do know the money's not important. This is spare change to the boss. There's something else, and whatever it is, it's worth more than Andy McVay's life."

"Look, why don't we wait till it's all settled down and go back there. We find out what they know. Maybe they have whatever it is and are hiding it?"

"Aarggh I just wanted to get out of this shit hole and go home."

Hillary gently unbuttoned his wet wool

coat, "You're so stressed, it's not good for your heart."

"Don't you go trying anything. I'm stressed because this job is fucked. It's not finished. We need to get our hands on that girl and start putting the pressure on." He tried to get up, but Hillary stopped him with a hand on his chest.

"It's late, and the police are everywhere. Why don't I help you relax, and then I'll help you recover whatever it is you're here for." She pulled both lapels open and ran a finger over his belt buckle. His hands relaxed behind his head. "Then, you can take me with you. Just for a while, then I'll make my own way. I just need a bit of help to get started." She pulled the strap of his belt out and revealed a little of his stomach.

He sighed, "I guess I could give you a lift, a few hundred miles maybe."

"I'd certainly appreciate it," Hillary replied as she got onto her knees beside him and popped his button. He opened one eye and reached for the back of her neck as she tugged his zip down.

Claire

"The boys are top to toe in one bed, and Irene's in the other. The only thing I've got left is this wee sleeping bag, that will have to do. I can't believe that's her sister..."

Claire pulled the living room door closed behind her, leaving Anna curled up on the sofa with Alice, staring at the wall, saying nothing at all.

"Jean, the police are going to turn up here soon. I don't know what to say."

"Tell them everything" Jean stopped searching in the airing cupboard and looked at Claire like she was mad.

"I can't, it doesn't work like that. I'm not getting into an abduction court case against the gypsies, and there's no way in hell I'm pointing out some gun-toting gangster. Neither will Anna."

"Someone's killed her Dad! You have to tell the police." Jean's voice is verging on a screech.

"Ssh, it's a lot more complicated than that, there's.." She stops short as Anna opens the door.

"It's late. We all need to get some sleep. Is it ok if I take Alice up beside me?"

"Of course it is, hen. Here this will keep

you warm enough for the night. If you're needing to stay longer, we'll figure something out in the morning."

Alice took the blue power rangers sleeping bag and dragged it behind her up the stairs, followed by Anna, then Claire. Jean flicked a tear away with her finger.

Anna

"Alice, you can go in my bed," Claire offered.

She shook her head and leaned in closer to Anna.

"She'll be ok beside me tonight," Anna replied, re-arranging the cushions and pillows on the floor. The three of them continued in silence, too sad and shocked and tired for words. When all the shuffling and wriggling was done, Anna listened to the others breathing, knowing they were all awake and dealing with their own pain quietly. She wanted to tell them all it would be ok, but for once in her life, she really didn't think it could be.

She heard their breathing deepen and slow, and she prayed they were falling asleep. She didn't want any more questions, or to try and give any more reasons. Her body was giving in to the night, her limbs were heavy and numb, and her brain was finally following. She welcomed sleep, but she was dreading waking up in the morning.

***

"Did you hear that?" Anna woke up to Claire leaning out of her bed and poking her arm.

"What?" She replied, groggy and confused.

"Listen..." they waited, breath drawn, for something to happen. Anna gasped when a rattle of the back door handle vibrated through the stillness of the house.

"Shit! Have they found us?" Claire whispered, tiptoeing to the door, close to Alice's head. A quiet knock followed.

"I'll go. " Anna said, "You stay in here with her, don't let her come down."

"What the hell Anna? Phone the police! It could be Ronin, or those guys have come to finish what they started, or..."

A tiny cracking noise on the bedroom window halted Claire. Anna slid away from Alice's sleeping body and looked out of the window. Below her, in the back garden, stood Christine, with a handful of gravel. She pointed at Anna, then the door.

"Thank god, it's ok. I'll let her in before she wakes the whole house up."

"Oh Anna, I'm so sorry about your dad," Christine hugged her tight, "You know he didn't have long, don't you?" Anna pulled away and nodded, looking at her feet. "I'm glad you got to see him. Before it was too late. I just wish it had been in better circumstances."

Anna laughed. It was awkward, nervous sounding. "That's a fucking understatement."

"I wish I'd put a stop to all this before it went too far."

"There's nothing you could of done. This was all his doing. His bad choices catching up with him. And everyone else." Anna's lip trembled, she ran her fingers through her hair, trying to drag the emotion away from her face.

"What happened in my house tonight? I'm not allowed back in there you know? It's a crime scene! They kept me in the cells, questioned me for hours, asking about Andy and my ties to Swindon. Fucking Swindon? All I did was let an old pal stay a few nights, now they've got me pinned as part of some gang or something." Christine looked over Anna's shoulder into the hall, "Where's wee Alice?"

"She's safe, she's asleep upstairs."

"Poor wee lassie. They were asking about her. The polis said a kid had been seen and social work would be getting involved."

Soft footsteps descended the stairs. Christine's expression said she'd said too much.

"Aw, my wee darling, I'm so sorry about your Daddy, come here," she stretched her arms out as her eyes filled with tears. Alice let herself be absorbed in Christine's arms.

"I don't want to go with social workers, can't I just stay with Anna?" She sobbed. "Dad said. He said you'd look after me." Her little face was blotchy, her puffy eyes streamed.

"I'm not old enough to look after a kid." Anna's voice was shaky, "They'll be able to find you a nice family to stay with, people who can give you a proper life. I can't do that." Anna grasped for the words to stop her crying. Christine rubbed her back, "Come on now, we don't need to make any decisions right now, everyone's tired and emotional."

Jean appeared in the hall, wrapped in a huge dressing gown and fluffy slippers, "Come on, guys, I know it's been a tough night, but if yous wake the twins up, we'll all be sorry."

"Sorry Jean, sorry for bringing all this to your door." Anna said, "It's just, can Christine stay here tonight too?"

"Aye, I'm no going to put her oot on the street, am I?" She pulled two bath towels from the airing cupboard, "Here, Chris, this is all I've got left, make yourself a bed on the sofa."

"Thanks doll, appreciated. Mind and lock the front door. And I'll just check the back."

As Jean tiptoed up the stairs, Christine checked the locks, then twice more. She opened a little gap at the side of the curtains, positioned herself with a view onto the street, and draped her fully clothed body with the towels.

"You two get some sleep, and we'll sort something out in the morning,"

Anna was glad to have someone else taking control; this was all way too much for her to comprehend.

CHAPTER NINETEEN

19

Jackson

"Will we get one of those big 'incident tents' that you see on the news?" Jamie asked, using air quotes. Jackson cringed and wiped the condensation from her window to assess the view of Christine's house - Blue and white police tape flapping in the wind, PC Davis with his back to the rain, huddled in the doorway.

"I don't know. With the other guy still on the lose, they might want to keep it on the down-low. Too much attention could ruin their case."

"What about the person who lives there, the weird woman with the gelled hair?

What did she say?"

"Christine? Nothing. Adamant she knew nothing about it and was out all night."

"And you believe that?"

"Of course I don't. Gangsters don't just shoot in each other in your house without you knowing something about it."

"Why did they let her go then? Can't we just keep her in till she spills the beans?"

Jackson sighs, and replies slowly and deliberately, "No, because she has an alibi, her presence at the bingo with her neighbour has been confirmed. We had to let her go."

"Why does this job have to be so hard? If it was up to me, I'd just say, 'listen hen, you're no going anywhere till you give us all the details, or you'll go to jail for it." He points his finger at an imaginary person.

"Me too Jamie, unfortunately, the Scottish legal system doesn't allow it, so we need to find evidence."

"Have we even found any yet?" Jamie asked, exhausted.

"The house is supposed to be sealed up till tomorrow, but I do have the other witness statement. An old boy that was walking his Collie, said he saw two adults and a child run across the road seconds before the gunshots. He's certain they were female, and I'll put money on one of them being Anna McVay."

"Shall we go and arrest her? Smith said she's staying in a house up in the estate."

"We can't just go steaming in, handcuffs swinging. Her father just got shot. We'll get a bit more to go on first, then question her tomorrow."

"Can we just go home then? You're not going to solve this by the morning."

"Once the CID take over in a couple of hours, we won't be allowed near this. Please, just a little while longer? I'll send Davis home, and you take over his spot at the door. You don't even need to do anything. Just stand there, and I'll do the rest. I'm going to look around again, then take a drive round via the Ashvale. I'm not handing over any info till I've had the chance to find the other one myself."

"You do know you'll get the sack when they find out? What you're doing goes against every single rule we have."

"I just need a couple of hours. Please?"

"I'm only joking. I don't even remember what rules we have. But I will be taking an umbrella and wearing my scarf and gloves if I'm standing on a bloody doorstep all night."

Jackson leaned in to hug him, then pulled back, surprised and embarrassed.

"Right, let's get to work then."

Anna

Upstairs, on the makeshift bed made of sofa cushions, Anna unzipped the bobbly sleeping bag and pulled it over both of them.

"I don't want to go with a social worker, I want to stay with you," she sobbed.

"Shh, don't wake everyone up. It will be ok. You'll get looked after by a nice family that can give you the things you need."

Her little eyelashes were stuck together, her eyelids puffy from crying.

"I could come and visit, we could write letters too, we won't lose touch, but I just can't look after you." Anna pulled the cover up to Alice's chin, her tears continued to roll, and a loud sob escaped.

Up on the bed, Claire rolled over. Her breathing was shallow; Anna wondered if she was awake, hoping she'd chip in and help subdue the hurting child.

"Why? Do you not like me?" Alice asked in the saddest voice she'd ever heard.

"No, it's not that. I'm just too young. I don't know how to look after a kid. I don't know how to do anything like that. And I don't have any money, kids need things like packed lunch boxes and wellies that fit, and dentist check-ups, and sun cream, and all that kind of stuff I don't know about." She leaned in closer and whispered extra quiet, in case Claire was actually awake, "and I don't even have a job. I got sacked, so there's no way I can look after you."

"What about the last tube?" Alice lifted the burgundy velvet cushion, slid out the damp map, and unfolded it. "Look, under the tree. Dad said do a big cross there coz it's the most important one. It's still there. Let's get it, and you'll have money, and you can look after me."

"We can't go back now. The police will be there, and Gina will be going crazy about her garden. No, it's gone. It's too late."

"Pleeeeeaa." Her plead was turning into a desperate cry, her little face twisting with sorrow.

"Sshhh," Anna stroked her head. She

needed to distract her before everyone was woken up.

"Hey, I've got a present for you, something special that I've had for a long time, that our dad gave to me," Anna whispered while leaning over and unzipping the pocket of her rucksack." I want you to have it now."

She fished out the delicate chain, still knotted and broken, with the thin gold pendant, and held it up in the light coming from the hallway. "It's a Saint Christopher."

"He looks after us, doesn't he?" Alice dried her eyes and watched it spin on the chain.

"yeah, Dad gave it to me when I was 10, and now you can have it. It might bring you luck."

Alice felt around her neck, into the tangled mess of hair around her shoulders, caught her own necklace, and pulled it over the top.

"I've got the same man on mine, but look, mine opens, it's a locket."

Anna opened the door a little more to get some extra light, and watched Alice's little fingers separate the gold edges and reveal the tiny photo inside. She couldn't see it clearly, but she knew immediately. Her face prickled, and a lump rose in her throat. That fringe, and the silhouette of her tie. It was Anna's primary six school photo, made impossibly small, encased in gold, kept safe by tiny hands, around the neck of the sister she never knew she had.

"You should keep yours, and we will both have the same. Like twins." Alice said, eyes getting heavy. Anna guided her head down, and tucked the sleeping bag under her side. She watched for a while as she floated off to sleep, looking at her face, so familiar but still so new.

Anna knew grief. She knew that when Alice woke in the morning, she'd be hit with it again. During the night, he could still be there. Anything was possible, then when she opened her eyes in the light of day, it would strike her again, like a punch in the stomach.

She slid off the cushions and lay flat on her back, listening to the slow rhythmic breath of her friend and new sister, trying to slow her own and force herself to sleep.

Anna

She'd lost her dad all over again. The first time had taken years. From expecting him to walk through the door at any second, to hoping he'd maybe turn up for a birthday or Christmas, to wondering if he was alive to regarding him as dead, she'd grieved in a distant, uncertain way.

Now he'd left all over again. From the moment he said he was sick, to the nod of acceptance back in that room, to hearing the gunshot, all within a couple of hours. Now she's lying in the dark, with a million feelings fighting to be felt.

She didn't want to feel any of them. She wanted to crack open a bottle of whisky and gulp away the emptiness. Memories of the days after her mum had died were leaking into her thoughts. A hot tear rolled backward into her ear.

That's what Alice had in store, weeks of agony, months of sorrow, years of living on the edge of anyone mentioning him and bringing it all back again. She'd have to do it alone, with a new family that didn't even know him. She wouldn't have the luxury of wondering if he was alive dull the blow over the years. She'd wake up every day alone, knowing for certain that he wasn't coming back. Alice wouldn't have that innocent hope that Anna had kept alive for years. She'd have nothing.

She rolled on her side, saw the rippled damp paper of the map with the big red cross in the middle.

The most important one. How much was left?

Maybe it was enough to keep Alice in school clothes and cornflakes for a few years. She made a list of the things she might need.

1, clothes for all kinds of things, indoor, outdoor, sleeping.

2, help with homework.

3, healthy food.

Then she thought of the things she'd really need. The things Anna had wished she'd had when she'd been left alone.

Someone to talk to when she felt like she didn't fit in with the friends she had.

Someone to tell her not to waste time on boys that tell you lies.

Someone to encourage her to find something she was interested in.

Someone to encourage her to say how she felt.

Someone to stand up for her, to be on her side no matter what.

She brushed a strand of hair from Alice's peaceful face, then shook her shoulder gently.

"Hey, wakey wakey, let's go and get our money." She whispered into her ear, "We're going to need it if you're coming to live with me."

CHAPTER TWENTY

20

Jackson

"Find anything interesting?" Jamie asked Jackson through chattering teeth when she returned from searching the back garden again.

She held up two plastic evidence bags filled with orange and black sludge.

"What the hell is that?"

"I don't know, but it's all over the back garden. It might be a sign of something."

Jamie took one and held the bag up towards the street light, spinning it around. He opened it and sniffed.

"It's burnt bloody fish fingers. Do you think it was a row about a burnt tea?"

Jackson sighed, disappointed, and peered into the bag. He was right.

"My batteries are done," she shook the torch, pressing the button repeatedly, hoping for a miracle.

"Can we go now then?" Jamie looked hopeful.

"I need you here a little while longer. I'm going to take the car and do a couple of circuits of the town, ok? I won't be long."

"Please be quick. I'm so cold, and tired. I feel like I might actually die of hypothermia. And, you know..."

"What?"

"Well, it's a bit scary. Just standing here, people were killed in there." He pointed at the wooden board covering Christine's front door.

Jackson shook her head.

She scanned the pavement and the surrounding area. She couldn't find anything notable. She was growing more and more frustrated.

"There must be clues, evidence, a better bloody witness! This is my town, I'm not just handing a double murder over to some Aberdonian wankers from Queen Street station as soon as they turn up. I've solved a gang murder before. I can do this one. We can do this. All you need to do is stand here till I get back!"

"Ok, ok, Christ's sake." Jamie huffed.

She got in the car and adjusted all the mirrors, making sure she had optimum visibility. She inspected the lines between her eyebrows, and the grey creased skin under her eyes. She looked exhausted, but she wasn't giving up.

She wound the window down as she drove, needing the fresh air to keep her awake. The town was empty, battered by the storm. A bin lay on its side on the High Street. Chip wrappers swirled with the wind. A solitary rat ran over the steps up to the Giles church in the center of town. Leaves blew down South Street. The Ashvale was in darkness. Everywhere was abandoned.

The post office, the bridge, the park, the library - of course nothing was happening! It was the middle of the night, in the middle of winter. What the hell did she expect? Criminals walking around looking to be questioned?

She slammed the steering wheel, she

knew it was time to give up and get some sleep, but she just couldn't drop it. In a few hours, she wouldn't be allowed anywhere near it. She'd just do one more circuit and go back for Jamie.

Ronin

He knew it was cold, but his rage was burning so deep he was hot as he marched towards Christine's house.

He'd been left in the dark, his van wedged up the lane, with no keys and only a flickering, dim interior light, searching for his gun. He'd felt around under the seats and in between. He'd searched in the mud on his hands and knees. He'd got in the back and fumbled around through the tools and rubbish, but he couldn't find it. The only thing of any use was a cricket bat, which he gripped in a tight fist, his arms straight by his side.

He was so furious, they'd have to shoot him in the head to stop him. He would punch, bite and rip the flesh from the bones of the men that took Hillary. He'd get their money back and finish off anyone that tried to stop him.

His teeth clenched so tight he felt a tooth crack. Pain seared through his jaw, and he growled in rage and agony. The wind stuck his wet shirt to his chest, it flapped behind him as he continued, stride unbroken, rain dripping from the ledge of his brow, on his way to get his woman back from the men who had humiliated him.

He'd walked miles through the streets. He'd been to the Ashvale, but the car was nowhere to be seen. Now he was getting closer to the house where the money had been buried. Someone would know where they were, and he'd do whatever it took to get that information out of them.

He walked faster and faster as he imagined smashing Anna's teeth out with his cricket bat. He'd happily flatten the old bitch Christine too. His lip curled as he imagined her skull cracking open.

Anna

"These are boy's wellies," Alice said, as they watch Christine's house from behind a bare beech tree, dressed in the first things they could grab on the way out of Jean's house.

In the few short hours since they heard the gunshots, the place has been sealed with chipboard, the gate and door taped off, and a policeman keeps watch on the doorstep.

"We'll never get past him. This is useless." Anna said

"We have to. Dad said it's the most important one."

"We should just wait, come back another day, once this is all over."

"But what if someone else finds it."

"It's just money. This is too dangerous. I don't know what I was thinking. Come on, let's get you safe."

"It's not just money. It's the real reason we came here."

"What do you mean, the real reason? What's under there?

"I don't know, but that's what Dad wanted us to find. And that's why those bad guys are after us."

The old familiar feeling of finding out she'd been lied to, her head began to shake from side to side automatically, she sighed. "And here was me thinking he really did come back to find me."

"Oh no, we did. He wanted me and you to

have whatever is in there."

"Whatever it is will have to stay there. We can come back another time, it's too cold and wet, and he's watching, come on." Anna didn't want to tell Alice that this was obviously one of Andy's giant promises - just another Disney land. She took her hand and backed away from the tree,

"But, Dad said,"

Anna turned away and pulled her, more firmly this time, she couldn't find the words, and the sadness was about to pour out.

Alice tugged her arm, "Look, he's going, the policeman's going away."

Hillary

Billy drove with the lights off, stopping at the top of the hill with a view down the street to Christine's.

"What are we even doing here? Let's just go. We can come back once the heat's off."

"Nonsense," Hillary squeezed his thigh, "if what you came for is still there, then it will be found tonight. I'd rather it was by us than Andy's lot, those girls, or the police. Wouldn't you? I mean, that is your job isn't it?"

"The place is boarded up. They don't do that unless someone's been knocked off. Fuck, it better be Andy and not Frankie."

"Indeed." Hillary said quietly as she used her sleeve to remove the growing condensation from the window.

"As long as that cop is standing there, we ain't going anywhere near, and neither will anyone else. Let's call it a night and wait to hear from Frankie. He'll be keeping his head down somewhere. He'll get in touch in the morning."

"Perhaps," She sighed as he was about to turn the key, "Look, wait, he's leaving," she batted his arm with the back of her hand. They watched the police officer close the gate, look up and down the street and pick up speed on the way down the hill.

Once he's out of sight, Billy reaches for the door handle but Hillary stops him once more with her hand. She points towards the edged of the park where Anna and Alice have emerged from the darkness. As they watch them run across the road and into the garden, Hillary smiles and says, "Let them do the dirty work, give them a head start, and we can finish it off."

He opens his mouth to answer, she stops him with her finger on his lips, "They can get their hands dirty, and we can reap the reward."

CHAPTER TWENTY-ONE

21

Anna

They watch Jamie fold his arms across his chest and walk down the hill, looking from side to side, his pace quickening to a jog. Then he was out of sight.

"Let's just try, for five minutes. Do you remember where it is? Coz I've got the map here." Alice offered the crumpled paper.

Anna looked up and down the road, scanning for any movement, or lights flicking on or off. Gina's house was in darkness, the upstairs curtains still open, telling Anna that she wasn't in. She'd probably come home to the chaos next door and taken herself off somewhere safe for the night, which is exactly what they should be doing, not heading right back into the mouth of the volcano.

She took a deep breath and shrugged, "Just five minutes, if we don't find anything, we're calling it quits before he comes back, ok?"

The wind had died down a little, but the rain was relentless. She lifted Alice over the gate in case it creaked, then she swung her legs over the rail.

The apple tree stood twice her height in the middle of the dark sodden lawn. In the far corner, the black pool created earlier, surrounded by clumps of mud, the flooding disguised by the torrential rain, Anna felt the freezing water rise up her jeans. The spade still stood, impaling the earth beneath the tree where she'd prepared to dig.

"Stand there, lean on the wall. Keep an eye out, tell me if you see anything, anyone at all, ok?" She couldn't tell where the rain stopped, and the snot started on Alice's face as she nodded, wide-eyed.

This area was harder than the others, the spade bounced off tree roots. She couldn't get a decent chunk out. She had to get small pieces, bit by bit, scraping along and in between the roots.

Then it felt different, smooth, hollow. She got on her knees, delved her hands into the black earth, feeling around, locating the end of the tube. She felt the dirt separate her nails from their beds, as she dug frantically, scraping away. She glanced quickly from Alice, to the hole, back and forth, checking her face for a sign of danger.

She pushed and pulled, felt her cuticles peel back and mud lodge beneath as she tried to free the tube from the gnarly fingered grip of the roots. She found the end, and dug in hard with her fingers.

"A car, there's a car coming," Alice shouted from her lookout position.

"Get down, come here, quickly." Anna said.

Alice dropped to the ground and crawled through the mud to Anna's side. Any reserve Anna had was abandoned; she was too close to give up now. She found the hard roots holding it in place and began wrestling with them. She curled her fingers underneath and yanked hard. One snapped. She wrapped both hands around the remaining root and pulled. She changed position and put her feet at either side, leveraging her weight and jerking till it gave, she fell backward.

A car door slammed.

She left the tube in the ground and dragged Alice backward towards the wall to hide them from the road. Alice squeaked. Anna put her finger to her mouth, warning. The gate creaked, Anna pulled her closer, she let out a tiny yelp, Anna covered her mouth with her hand. Feet bounded the stairs. Anna closed her eyes tight, wishing to dissolve into dust and be washed away down into the ground. She could feel Alice's hot face under her palm, her body tense. Thunder rumbled in the distance.

Claire

Claire stood still in the kitchen. She'd heard them leave the room and followed close behind; she wouldn't sleep knowing they were out there.

She could see Christine in the living room, facing the street, her face lit by the gap in the curtains. With her eyes closed, she looked younger without the lines of worry that shaped her during the day.

She took a sip of someone else's glass of water. It was warm, but she didn't want to risk the noise of running the tap for a fresh one.

She put her hand to her chest, feeling the thump of her heart beatr through her ribs. She asked herself the same question that had been running through her head continually.

Why did we have to come back here?

All of this could have been avoided. Everything was fine; life was good. She felt like screaming. The beat under her hand was irregular, she felt the sweat prickle on her back, trying to get her breath under control, all she could hear was the crack of her heart inside its cage.

She felt a hand on her shoulder. Her mum stood close in the dark, she pulled her nearer. For the first time in years, Claire didn't tense, she melted into her arms and allowed the warmth to spread.

Her mums' breath was slow and steady, it calmed Claire in a way that felt familiar but hazy - a memory buried deep, crushed under piles of resentment.

As her mum rubbed her back, the feeling

of her hand sparked memories. There had been times when this exact hug from her mum made everything ok.

"You could stay up here," Irene whispered, "We could get a house together, we could start again, be a real family."

Claire pulled away, looking into her mum's eyes, looking for a flicker of truth. "You and me? Together?"

Irene nodded, then shrugged it off, "It's fine if you don't want to, I understand. Never mind." She turned her head away, Claire saw the glimmer of tears balancing on her lower eyelids.

"It's not that. It's just, well, a lot has happened. My life's in Edinburgh now."

"It's fine, honestly," Irene pulled away and backed into the hall, "forget I said anything, it was silly."

Claire stayed there, rooted to the floor, watching her mum, the one she used to know, walk up the stairs, sad and rejected. She took a cigarette out of Jean's packet and slipped out of the back door.

She'd been stopping for a few months, got down to one every couple of days, but she needed to smoke now more than ever.

Sitting on the cold step, she felt the damp

seep into her nightie; she hugged herself tight against the wind and listened to the thunder rumbling closer each time.

Anna

Lashing rain washed the mud from the white plastic. It shone like a full moon in the middle of the dark garden. Anna held Alice tight, hand over her mouth, blocking the scream that bubbled underneath.

He stood tall, towering above them. His eyes darting between the unearthed tube and Anna, cowering in the mud, protecting her little sister.

"Now, I'm going to take this," he stepped towards the tube, unsteady on the slippery lawn, "and you two are going to forget you ever met me, ok? Or I'll come back and finish you both off."

Alice pulled free, scrambled across the mud, and threw herself towards it, "No, it's ours, get away, you horrible man!" she screamed.

His foot crushed down on top of her tiny fingers. Anna crawled across and pushed his knee, trying to release her. He punched the side of her head, she reeled backward, elbows splashing in the freezing water. Alice was still trapped, crying in anger and pain.

Anna froze, watching Hillary's expression change as she reached inside her coat, pulled out an ancient-looking gun, and swung it in their direction. Anna threw herself in front of Alice, pushing on Billy's shin. She closed her eyes, waiting for the shot, desperately pushing and pulling to release Alice's hand from beneath his foot.

"Get your foot off that child's fingers immediately!" Hillary shouted. He dismissed her with one look, and grabbed a handful of Anna's hair.

"Now!" Hilary stepped forward and pushed the back of his head with the barrel. "Let go of her and step away."

Hillary stepped back out of his reach; he lifted his foot slowly. Alice scuttled backward with the tube, and Anna remained on her knees.

Billy straightened his back, taking in the whole scene. He smiled in disbelief and shook his head.

"Now, now, sweetheart. Don't you be getting all excited."

"Get on your knees, over there." She pointed the gun towards the hole filled with dark water in the corner. He shook his head and laughed, leaning back down for the tube.

"Don't you dare." Her tone was hard; he heard the difference. "Girls, take that tube and get out on the pavement. You, put your fucking hands up. Now!"

Alice wrapped both arms across her chest, with the tube held tight inside. Anna slid to her feet, shielding her sister on the way.

"Give me the keys," Hillary held her hand out, he shook his head.

"Don't think so, sweetheart." He sneered. Hillary rolled her eyes and sighed. She pulled the trigger, shooting the mud by his feet.

"Keys! Now get on your fucking knees!"

He handed the keys over, and she kept a steady aim on his head.

"Now, lie down, and bloody stay there." Hilary walked backward out the gate, still aiming at him, becoming aware of lights going on in surrounding houses, realising the noise she'd just made.

"Up the hill girls, get in that blue car. Chop, chop."

Alice scrambled into the back seat, Anna clipped her seat belt in, and Hillary handed her the gun.

"Roll the window down and point it towards him. If he tries to stop us, just shoot him, got it?"

Anna nodded, she'd never held a gun before, but she felt oddly safe with it in her hand. Whether she was capable of pulling the trigger or not, she had no idea. As they sped past the houses at the bottom of the hill, Anna saw him rise from behind the wall.

"Thanks," Anna began, hesitating, waiting for the approaching car to pass them.

"Well, I wasn't about to stand by and watch a grown man be cruel to a child, was I?"

Brake lights from the passing car lit up the mirrors. Hillary sped up a little, watching the reverse lights illuminate behind them. She didn't show any alarm as she quickly weaved through parked cars and down onto the main road.

"We really appreciate it, don't we?" Anna looked round to check on Alice, then asked, "What happened back at the house, to our Dad? Did you see?"

Hillary looked in the rear-view mirror,

tilting it to see Alice's reflection. She smiled kindly when she caught her eye.

"I don't know, girls, I ran just after you. I was terrified, I heard the shots, but I don't know what happened."

"He's dead. They both are. The police told Christine."

Jackson

Jackson drained the sticky drips of yesterday's sugary coffee from her flask and rubbed her eyes. It was time to give up. The remaining suspect was long gone, or smart enough to stay hidden. She'd go back and relieve Jamie, then take the post herself for the next couple of hours. At least if she was on the scene when the CID turned up, she'd get another look inside. She'd hopefully be able to demonstrate that her local knowledge was needed.

She felt a creep of guilt pulling its way up inside her stomach. She still hadn't told any of her superiors about the call from Swindon. Those English guys would be turning up soon, and she'd need to explain why she hadn't passed on any information.

A chill grew up the back of her neck. This could be the end of her career. It wouldn't matter how well operation Brown Owl had gone, or how quiet the town had been for the last six months; she hadn't followed instructions or procedure.

Who on earth would she be without this uniform?

She'd never wanted to be anything else. Thunder rolled in the distance. As she wound up the window, an extra loud crack of thunder made her jump. Jamie would not be enjoying this; she laughed a little at the thought of him wincing at the noise.

The wiper blades swished across the glass, and the heater blew dry air at her face. She started feeling sleepier and sleepier, hypnotized by the repetitive sound and the rising temperature.

Arriving back the scene, a car passed with no lights on. She braked, changed gear into reverse, ready to pursue. As she skidded backward and hit the kerb, she saw a tall man standing in front of the houses, wearing a long dark coat. It was him! The other Swindon man! She didn't turn the engine off, just jumped out of the car and ran towards him, he took off up the hill, she followed.

"Jamie! Help!" she shouted as she passed his abandoned post. "Useless idiot" she panted.

He was getting away, his legs were longer and stronger. But, she knew this town, every lane and doorway, every building and street, if he was on foot, she'd catch him eventually.

She ran, determined, finding energy from deep inside. An emergency call came through her radio, it was too windy to hear, and she couldn't stop to respond. She was losing ground. He was approaching the top of the hill, between parked cars and into the light, Jackson followed course, pushing with the last bit of energy she had before she would lose him into the darkness of the park.

A figure was approaching from the tree line, thinly clothed, in a light shirt, swinging a weapon of some kind.

Jackson halted, her breath stopped, feet welded to the spot, the wind whipping her wet hair across her open mouth.

A Dougherty brother, unmistakable. He stopped her man, floored him with one swing of his weapon. Her mark was now on his knees, collapsing onto one hand, holding his head with the other. The Dougherty swung the bat in both hands, with a force she thought might take his head off.

"Stop! Police!" She shouted, her single set of handcuffs ready to lock the wrists of one of them. But only one.

He wasn't stopping for her or anything else. The bat swung heavily and cracked against the side of his head; he crumbled the last few inches to the ground, consciousness gone.

"Stop! Stop! Police! You are under arrest!" She shouted, breathless, resting her hands on her thighs to regain some strength. She held out her single pair of handcuffs, weighing up her choices as time stood still.

Her radio crackled again, now standing still, she could make out words… firearms… response… Green Street…

In the distance, a siren wailed. On the ground, her mark began to stir, moving up onto his elbows, groaning.

She looked in Ronin's wild eyes under his dark brow. He placed his foot between Billy's shoulder blades, pushing him down.

Jackson snapped the cuffs on behind his back and forced him onto his knees. He groaned, and his head sagged forward, a river of blood spread across the side of his face, helped along by the rain.

Ronin stepped backward, as the sirens got louder, he receded into the darkness. Jackson looked away. She didn't acknowledge him, his help, or his departure. Well, no one needed to know, did they?

The blue strobes in the misty wet air lit the way as she proudly presented her prize to the newly assembled officers. Jamie patted her shoulder, "Well done." He whispered.

"Where the hell were you?" she mumbled from the side of her mouth.

"I was just so bored and freezing, I went home, but I only got a wee bit down the road, and my stupid radio started going off. I ran back here so I didn't get in trouble."

"And what did you see?"

"I saw you, chase down and catch this awful criminal."

"That's correct, Jamie, and you didn't leave your post all night."

"That's correct," He smiled as he pulled his woolly hat down over his ears and put his police hat on top. "But, what do you think really happened?"

"Hmm, I reckon this guy shot the other two, and he was coming back to get rid of the evidence."

"Are you going to be in trouble? For not telling anyone about them being here?"

"A bit maybe, but I think that one in cuffs will give me a bit of leeway. Let's get some rest now, then first thing, we'll bring Anna and her friends in for questioning."

CHAPTER TWENTY-TWO

22

Anna

"Oh lord, can you hear that? More sirens. We need to get as far away from here as possible." Hillary was driving carefully, indicating her every turn and staying below the speed limit.

"I can't. We need to go back and get Claire. I'm not leaving her here. Turn right, up there, into the second street."

"You can come back for her, right now, I need to leave this place, and I'm the one driving."

"Let us out now then, stop the car."

"Don't be so hasty. The police will be looking for all of us, especially you. It was your father that brought all this about." Hillary said.

"Well, what the hell are we going to do?" Anna asked.

"I don't want to go away with the social workers. I want to stay with you." Alice sobbed in the back. Anna reached round and rubbed her knee, "Don't worry, you're staying with me. Just put your head down and try and rest a bit."

Hillary slowed the car and pulled into a narrow space next Roy's Spar. She jumped out and pulled a trolley of empty bread crates in front of the number plate and kicked some empty crisp boxes around the sides.

She got back in and faced Anna. They sat in silence for a while, letting Alice drift off, checking the mirrors, and listening for cars or feet approaching.

"I'm not quite sure how things have gotten so far out of control, but I'm hoping you and I can both benefit from this evening's events."

"Benefit? How? My Dad's dead, you're going to jail, and" she mouthed the rest silently, "she's probably going into care."

Hillary pointed in the back, to the green

leather bag under Alice's sleeping head. All the money is in that bag, and well, whatever's in that last one," Alice held the tube tight in her arms, unrelenting even in sleep.

"It's your money, isn't it? I mean, your father meant it for you, and her. I could have disappeared with it, but I saved you both, and I'm willing to share."

"It's poisonous that money, it's bad news. Whatever trouble happened for him to end up with it, it followed him. It ruined my life because he couldn't come back. It ruined his life because he had to live in fear, always watching his back and now it's ruined hers. She's just a kid, but she doesn't know what it's like just to play, be free to run about outside. He's kept her hidden for fear of whatever he's done coming back to haunt them."

"What will you do then? When the police want to take her away? They'll put her in a home, you know, or perhaps foster care."

Anna's lip trembled and a tear rolled down the side of her nose. "I promised her that wouldn't happen. I don't know what to do."

"The only thing we can do, we take the

bloody money and get out of here." Hillary laughed, "It's not like you haven't done it before."

Anna's mouth turned downward, hot tears ran from both eyes. "Oh my god, I'm just like him. I'm just as bad. I'm going to spend my life hiding from my past, just like him."

"You're not like him, Anna, you know what's important. How you look after that little girl is what's important."

Anna wiped her tears with the side of her hand and took a big breath in to steady her heart.

"I need to get back to Edinburgh, to my flat. I'll take her with me. But I need to get Claire. She lives with me. I can't just leave her here after what she's been through the last few days. I can't believe she's been dragged into my trouble again."

"Well, I've been waiting for a way out of this dump for a long time. Ronin promised me that, again and again. I'm sorry about what happened to your friend, tying her up wasn't my idea. It was obviously you that was supposed to be abducted."

"What the fuck Hillary?" Anna looked at her in horror.

"Kidding, kind of. Anyway, it's all worked out now, hasn't it? We've got the money, and the bad guys are all taken care of."

"Except Ronin. He'll be looking for this car, wont he?

"Oh shit. Yes, he will. Ok, change of plan, where did you say your friend is?"

"Just up there, the next street."

"Wake up, little one, time to get moving! We're going on a little adventure."

"Is it morning?" Alice mumbled.

"Not yet," Anna pulled her out and hoisted her onto her hip, still gripping onto the tube.

Hillary rummaged in the green bag for a second, then lifted it onto her shoulder. She produced a small tin of Elnett hair spray and then a lighter from her pocket. Aiming at the pile of newspapers and sandwich boxes in the back foot-well, she lit the spray and ignited the back of the car with a big smile. She chucked the tin into the fire,

"Chop chop girls, lead the way!"

Anna and Alice stared, open-mouthed as the flaming car lit up the street.

Hillary moved behind them, herding them along. Alice giggled, "She's crazy."

Alice bounces on Anna's back as they swerve into the path at the side of Jean's house. They stop to catch their breath.

"Shh, you'll have to stay back here until I explain to Claire. She'll freak out when she sees you. Give me two minutes, and I'll sort it out,"

Anna entered the garden to see Claire sitting on the step blowing smoke in her direction, "Who? Who will freak me out?" she stands up, gripping the fabric of her top, stepping back toward the door. Anna puts one hand up, gesturing her to keep calm, while holding Alice on her hip with the other.

"It's Hillary, you know, Mrs thingy. She helped us, we got all the money and the other tube, but now it's got a bit worse, so we need to go."

"Worse? How? How could anything be any worse?" Claire's pitch rose with each word.

"Sshh, don't wake everyone up. It's complicated. It's just..."

"Complicated, oh my god you sound like your Dad.

"I can't explain out here. We need to get in

and hide."

Hillary slowly appeared from the corner, smiling sweetly at Claire.

"That woman is not welcome in this house." Claire said to Anna, looking straight at Hillary.

"That woman saved us. We could be dead by now, but she saved us. Come on. We need to get Alice inside. She's freezing."

Behind Claire, the kitchen door creaked open, Christine placed a gentle hand on her shoulder and said, in a firm voice.

"Everybody get inside. The bairn's freezing."

As they filtered through the door into the safety of the house, an explosion rattled the dished in the sink. Not the sharp bang of a gun, but a duller, bigger bang that shuddered their rib cages. Christine ran to the front window, making a gap in the curtains with her thumb and finger. She turned to the rest of the room, then opened them up as far as her arms would stretch. The view beyond a was silhouette skyline of shed roofs and bare trees, lit from behind by a raging fire.

"Whit the fuck is that?" Christine looked straight at Anna this time. Anna looked at

Hillary. Christine closed the curtains again, shaking her head.

"The polis are going to be here before the sun's even up. I spent half the night in the polis station getting grilled about a fucking double murder in ma hoose. Now you've went oot and dragged this liability of a woman here, and managed to blow up the next fucking street."

Alice buried her face into Anna's side; she gave Christine a look begging her to stop.

"You's are all suspects. You, wee Claire and this one," she pointed at Hillary, "And the polis will be here, sooner rather than later."

"We're not suspects. They shot each other," Anna said, looking confused.

"Look, I've no idea what happened back there, but the polis seem to think there's a lot more than those two, shot for shot."

"Em, can I just suggest," Hillary interrupted, "that we perhaps leave, as soon as possible?"

"Aye, I think you should," Christine said, nodding at Hillary.

Anna closed her eyes and pulled air deep into her lungs, "Let's all go. If we aren't here, no one can ask anything. We can go back to

Edinburgh."

"We don't have a car, remember," Alice said, pointing towards the window and the fire beyond.

"What about Jean's car?" Anna suggested.

Claire choked on air, and laughed, "No way, not this time, she'll go crazy. She only just got the insurance money to buy this one."

"Perhaps we could reimburse her? Make it worth her while?" Hillary said as she peeled a bundle of notes from a roll.

As they all stared at the money in Hillary's hand, the wail of the fire engine approached, still in the distance but getting clearer.

"We need to go. Everyone get your stuff, quickly," Anna said.

"I'm going nowhere." Christine started, "I've said my bit to the polis, I'm running from no one. But, I could do with some reimbursement for the state of my house." Her voice was steady as she held her hand out towards the roll of cash. Anna took it from Hillary's grip and put it in Christine's. She felt the weight, then pulled Alice over, and the three of them hugged.

Hillary and Claire looked away from each

other.

"I don't want to be rude, but we really need to get cracking," Hillary said.

Anna relaxed her arms, Christine let go. As they separated, a rare tear dropped from Christine's eye.

"Claire, get the keys and let's go," Anna said.

Claire looked at the floor and shook her head slowly.

"Come on, Jean will be ok. There's ten times what the cars worth there."

Claire didn't look up. She picked the bunch from the wooden bowl on the sideboard, unwound the black fob, then held it out to Anna, still not making eye contact.

"I'm not coming, just you go."

Anna grabbed her arm, shaking it gently, "You have to, don't be scared, let's go."

Claire pulled her arm free. "I'm staying here, to be with my mum. She's changed. She said she wants to be a family again."

"But what about Edinburgh, our life there?"

"If your mum came back and asked you to stay, what would you do?" Claire looked up this time, straight into Anna's eyes, and she returned it with a smile, and her eye's welled up.

"What about the police? What will you say to them?"

"I'll just say I don't know anything. I was here all night, doing jigsaws with my mum."

"No, I mean about why we left in the first place. Will you be ok? What if you have another panic attack? I won't be there. What if the stress gets too much?"

"Don't worry," Claire put her calming hand on Anna's arm, "I know I've got some stuff to work through, but I'm leaving that in the past. The shit I've been through in the last 48 hours, I can handle a few questions."

Anna took the bag from Hillary's hand, reached in, and gave Claire a roll.

"I love you. I'll miss you."

"I'll miss you too, but I've got to give it a go. We've got another chance to be a family. I have to take it. And so do you. You've got a family now, you and your wee sister."

The sirens stopped a street away. Blue flashes lit up the smoke-filled night as they stuffed a duvet in the back of Jean's red Golf, making a cozy nest for Alice.

Hillary adjusted the seat and mirrors. Christine leaned into the window, and whispered a warning, "You better look after they girls."

Anna and Claire hugged. Claire pulled away when a light came on upstairs in the house, "Go, quick, before Jean comes down, I'll sort it out with her," she walked quickly without looking back.

Christine watched them leave, unblinking, arms folded.

They passed the smoldering car, past a fire engine and a police van. They made their way slowly past delivery trucks on the High Street, and overtook a milk van, easily blending in with the early morning signs of life.

Anna took in the familiar sights, the scratched peace sign on a door, the old sticker on the lamp post, the ragged posters for gigs long gone, and she knew this time, she'd never see them again.

Ronin

The searing pain of his broken tooth woke him up, and the memory of the night before punched him in the head before he even opened his eyes. Hillary was gone, the money was gone, his chance to hand McVay over to his family was gone. Anna, the thieving wee rat, got away again. His van was abandoned, and the gun was lost somewhere.

He swept his arm across Hillary's side of the bed with a little bit of hope that maybe she'd crept in during the night. But it was just him and his cricket bat.

At least he had that. One tiny fragment of success. He recalled his swinging arms, the heavy wood making contact with flesh. He'd given him a chance, but all he'd said was Hillary was gone. No explanation, no destination, nothing, so he'd cracked his skull. Again, and again. It felt good, a remedy for the frustration of being disrespected.

He put back on the damp jeans from the night before and smiled at the browning blood streak across the thigh. He took them off and put on his old jogging bottoms, they were a couple of inches too short, but they were dry.

There was no spare key for his van, but now it was daylight he could open up the dashboard and fire it up with just the wires. With a screwdriver in his pocket, and a dry shirt on, he tried to avoid the puddles on the track out of the site. He felt fragile and tense. Cold water splashing on his exposed ankles was pushing him to the edge.

The air smelt like the day after bonfire night, smoky and damp.

He planned to walk the longest, widest route to his abandoned van. He'd avoid the police station and the scene of last night's carry-on. That policewoman had let him go because she had no option. He wouldn't have heard the last of it.

He'd be dragged in for questioning soon, about the gunshots, the girl he tied up, the money he stole, the man whose skull he smashed in.

He tried to place the events in order, make some sense of his part in it all, but he couldn't. He needed to find Hillary first. She'd know.

He quickened his pace as a whistle beckoned him from behind.

"Hoi, Ronin! Wait for us!" Maria shouted.

He stopped and waited for them to catch up, dreading what they had to say.

"Looking sharp today pal," Tina giggled

as they looked him up and down.

"Did you hear what happened last night?" Maria asked.

"With the McVay's?" Tina added.

"Me? No, I didn't hear anything, nothing at all. Look, I've got to go, things to do."

Tina and Maria looked at each other and raised their eyebrows. "Well, uncle James is looking for his gun. It's missing."

"I can't help you. I've got to go. I've not heard anything." He noticed he was pulling his ear, and they were watching. The girls exchanged that look, the one that always led to trouble. He had to get away from them before he said anything. He walked away fast, feeling their accusing eyes burning into his back.

He squeezed between wet conifers and jaggy bramble thorns, sliding up the side of his van, into the driver's door. He could still smell Hillary's special perfume, just faintly, but it tugged his heart. He pulled the ignition cover off, with the skills he'd learned years ago, used the screwdriver to arrange the wires, and start the engine.

He resumed his search for the gun once more, outside and in. He checked the footprints in the mud, and the tire tracks made by their escape.

He got on his knees and looked underneath.

Inside, he ran his hands under the seats, between the cracks and down by the armrests.

He pushed his fingers down into the crumb-filled cavities where the seat belt holders were bolted.

There was something there. He slid onto the seat to weigh it down; the gap opened easily as the springs compressed. Something was down there. It wasn't his gun, but a roll of cash. A fat, heavy roll of hundred-pound notes. A stray one, looked over and forgotten, hiding there just for him.

He peeled back a corner and ran his nail around the top of the roll. Thousands and thousands of pounds.

If he didn't find Hillary, this would at least be some compensation.

It's not as if they were that close, really.

She was probably fine.

She'd come back if she wanted to.

Probably best if he didn't tell anyone about the money.

Or anything else.

He reversed out of the lane and drove down to the junction at the edge of town.

Left, back to the site, to his life of disappointment, frustration, trouble, ridicule, and losing all this money again. Or right, towards the bridge out of town, away from all of that, and towards the unknown.

He bounced on his seat and pulled his earlobe, just once. Then spun the wheel to the right, and put his foot down.

CHAPTER TWENTY-THREE

23

Anna

Anna blinked the grit from her eyes and rubbed a tight muscle in her neck; she must have slept for a couple of hours. The sky was blue and the air crisp as they crossed the Forth road bridge, last night's storm left long behind them.

"You'll need to direct me from here, I'm not familiar with Edinburgh."

A million thoughts flooded Anna; she opened the window for air as the gravity of her new situation sank through her stomach.

"Are you ok?" Hillary asked.

"Yeah, it's just, a lot to take in. I left here a couple of days ago, and everything was fine.

Now my entire life has flipped on its head."

"I am sorry about Andy. For your loss."

"This might sound bad, but honestly, I'll be ok. I've already grieved for him over the years. It's Alice I'm worried about."

"Will you be arranging his funeral?"

"Christine's getting him cremated, then we will do something special with his ashes. She's too young to go to a funeral, and anyway, God knows who'd turn up, we could all end up getting shot."

"It's all very mysterious, isn't it? I mean, why would a couple of gangsters want to get rid of a sweet little girl?

"I don't know. I think it was just to threaten him, force him to hand over the money."

"What about the other thing? Did he give you any clues as to what's in there?"

Anna looked at Alice's rosy cheeks, hair sticking to the side of her face as she stirred in her duvet nest on the back seat. She was still holding the tube like a favourite teddy bear. The mud was dry now and flaking off the ends.

Anna had already made up a list of improbable possibilities, but the one thing she knew for sure, was that it was private.

Something just for her and Alice, they'd open it together, alone, when the time was right.

"What will you do now?" Anna asked.

"Um, I have options."

"That's good." The car went quiet. Hillary opened her mouth to say something, then stopped. Anna took a breath to begin, but she hesitated. She looked out of the side window. Hillary coughed. Anna tried again,

"There's room at mine. For a night or two. If you need to get on your feet. No pressure, I mean if you don't want to, or if that's too weird."

"I suppose that would be useful. Short term, of course, while I weigh my options up."

The relief was palpable; they both smiled a little, and looked at Alice, sleeping soundly, on her way to her new life.

CHAPTER TWENTY-FOUR

24

Jackson

"Here's to Operation... eh, what was it again?" Jamie asked, holding up a paper cup full of glowing orange punch.

"Shh, keep it down." Jackson lifted her cup to meet his, "Project Wild Cat, but it was unauthorised. The name was just for me and you. No one else can know."

"My lips are sealed. Cheers! To you and your hunches."

"Cheers!" The paper cups folded slightly when they connected.

"Jamie, I was wondering. Would you like to be promoted? Away from the desk and out on the street with me? We make a good team."

"Not being funny, but actually, no."

"Fine, I was kidding anyway. As if I'd want you asking stupid questions all day." Jackson sipped and watched the rest of the party. The neck of her woolly Christmas tree jumper was beginning to itch.

"So, did forensics ever come up with anything in that garden?" Jamie asked.

"Nope, just a broken pipe and a botched fixing job. I had my hopes on a body being found, but nothing. Just a few muddy holes and nothing suspicious."

"And what're our English friends saying about it all?"

"They were very happy with me, delighted in fact. They'd been after that guy for a long time. If they can't pin any of this on him, they've a string of other hits and robberies he's wanted for."

"Pin this on him? The shootings? Didn't they shoot each other?"

Apparently not. Frankie De'Coza was shot by a third person, from a different angle. They don't have the gun, but reckon it's an old pistol. They pulled an ancient brass bullet out of his skull.

"Well, I'd put money on it being something to do with those lassies, Anna or her pal Claire." Jamie held out a gold cracker, shaking it till Jackson accepted the other end.

"Don't be daft," She laughed, "That pair are just kids. It's nothing to do with them."

She pulled; it cracked with a weak fizz. Jamie fished out a purple paper hat, unfolded it, and placed it on top of her head.

Claire

Claire has two envelopes; she's heading for the post box next to Roy's spar.

Someone's tried to paint over the black singed marks on the wall, but it just looks worse. Tiny bits of melted plastic are still welded to everything within ten meters.

It's been a couple of weeks now, but she hasn't ventured further than the end of this road.

She looks at the addresses on the envelopes, and pops just one of them in the slot. It was time to get on with her life, make the most of her second chance. She lit a cigarette, and carried on walking, slow and careful, still watching her back.

The further she walked, the more confident she grew. She'd dealt with the police interviews. She'd played the part well; they weren't interested in her.

No one had seen Ronin since that night. She'd been through the worst, and she was on the other side. She knew where she had to go now.

Her old street, the tiny house she'd loved, and the place she'd killed her father. She had to walk past it to see how she felt. She expected sweat, jelly legs, and a thumping chest. But, it was ok. Someone else lived there now, a candle burned in the window, and fake snow was sprayed in the corners inside.

The blood would be gone, her things long disposed of, and the memory of that night could fade away along with the rest.

She kept walking, through familiar streets, over the saggy fence, across a well-used shortcut to her last stop. She was about to slip the envelope through the letterbox, but decided to knock instead.

The door opened a few inches, enough to see half a grey face.

"Hi Wendy, Merry Christmas! This is from Bazz. He sends his love." She passed the envelope into her skinny hand.

Wendy shook it, and her face lit up. She dug a long-nailed finger under the flap and ripped it open; three shredded pieces floated to the ground, she flipped the card open. She thumbed through the corners of the notes inside.

"Four hundred quid? Merry fucking Christmas Doll." Wendy laughed.

"You know what you need to do, yeah?" Claire asked.

"I'll be at the next visit." She doesn't look up, she's counting the money again.

"Look after yourself, Wendy," Claire said, happy to see the genuine joy on her face.

Bazz

Bazz lies on his back, measuring the width of his bicep between his thumb and fingers. It's definitely bigger than last week.

"Mail." An officer shouts from the door and throws in two envelopes. He picks them up and sniffs. He lingers on the green envelope longer, breathing deep and savoring the smell of Charlie Red, running his finger over Wendy's curly handwriting.

The other, he's not too sure of. He hasn't

had any post from anyone else, so it makes him a little nervous. He tries to guess by looking at it, and holding it up to the light.

The top has already been opened and checked, so he decides to stop being silly and just pull the card out.

On the front, it read 'Christmas Wishes to a Wonderful Friend,' inside, written in gold pen are the words,

'Thank you for everything. I think about what you've done for me every day, and I appreciate it more than you will ever know. I have put some money in your property and popped a little gift in to Wendy in your name. If you need anything, please, just ask. Love Claire."

Claire

"Help me in with this shopping, hen." Jean shouted from the drive. Claire put her arms out at the boot of Jean's new white BMW, and she loaded her up with bags. Christine arrived in the drive, her lips blue and thin face shivering.

"Just checking whit yer needing me to bring over the morn?" She asked.

"Just yourself hen, and whatever you're drinking," Jean replied.

"You'll never guess," Christine began, as Jean balanced another box on Claire's arms. "I seen Gina yesterday. She's still raging about her garden. Thinks it's awffy suspicious that folk get murdered, and her garden gets wrecked the same night. I telt her, gangsters don't have time to gig up your tulip bulbs on the way for a fucking shoot-out, but she wouldn't shut up about it. So, I have to take her to the bingo every bloody week! Noo she's ma best pal. I fucking hate her fur what she did to ma Gizmo. God rest his soul."

"At least it's just Gina and not the polis." Jean replied, hanging another bag from Claire's finger.

"You've went a bit overboard, have you not?" Claire laughed.

"Well, I think we all deserve a good Christmas after the shit we've been through this year. Don't you? And, since your mum's here and Christine's coming round, I thought I'd better get extra.

In the kitchen, Claire arranged the shelves in the cupboards to fit in all the extra snacks.

The twins hovered around, desperate to get something.

"Here, take a couple of biscuits till I get this done," Claire said, offering them a packet of Bourbons. They tried to open it between them, pushing and pulling till it burst, brown shards and crumbs scattered across the floor.

Claire scooped them up onto a plate and handed them to the boys. They run upstairs, leaving the kitchen quiet again. Irene sat at the dining table, next to the jigsaw they'd been trying to finish.

"You're really good with those kids. So patient." She said, smiling at Claire.

"Thanks," she replied, angling the brush under the washing machine to remove the smashed bits of biscuit.

"Hey, look!" Claire picked something up and blew the fluff off. "It's the missing piece." She stood at her mum's side, and pressed the little bit of blue sky into the puzzle. "There we go, sorted."

CHAPTER TWENTY-FIVE

25

Anna

Alice stood on her tiptoes, hanging the third stocking above the fire.

"I'm not sure Santa's going to bring Hillary anything after she blew up that car." she laughed.

"Well, I think getting all our money back, and saving your fingers, and keeping the last tube made up for that," Anna said.

"When are we going to open it?" Alice asked for the three hundredth time.

"I just want it to be the right time, that's all."

"Christmas eve is the right time, I think." Alice sat cross-legged on the floor, her eyes reflecting the twinkling fairy lights from the tree.

Every day they had come up with new ideas about what could be sealed inside. Some completely impossible, but most just really unlikely. Diamonds, the deeds to their own haunted mansion, and a family tree showing their royal heritage and proof of their right to the throne were some of her favourites.

"Ok, let's see what the big fuss was about." Anna said.

Alice skipped through to the bedroom, returning to the stone hearth with the white plastic tube. Anna lifted the heavy brass door stop from the entrance and met her back on the rug.

Anna knew that once the secret was out of the tube, it was the end of the chapter. The mystery was keeping their Dad alive. The hours spent talking about him, making up stories, and dreaming up possibilities would be over. The little bit of magic stopping him from fading away would disappear.

"Go on. Just do it!" Alice said, full of excitement.

Anna held the weight high, and let it drop on the end. It cracked a little. She hit it again. The crack widened.

There was no magical golden light, no jewels pouring out, just two more rolls of cash, and a little yellowed, curled-up envelope.

There was no name on it. She held it up to the light and gave it a shake.

"Open it!" Alice said.

Anna peeled the edge away and tipped the contents on the rug between them.

A tiny silver key, attached with string, to a brown luggage tag. She held the tag up and read it. Alice's eyes were fixed on the key that dangled and spun beneath.

"What does it say?"

"0074593,SW7 1, 020 7581 1212, A M."

"What does it mean?"

"I have no idea." And she was glad. The mystery was still alive. She wasn't sure she wanted to know at all. Anna took the little key off the string, and added it to Alice's chain. It hung around her neck, close to her heart, next to the gold St Christoper locket, that held the tiny photo of her big sister.

Printed in Great Britain
by Amazon